To my brother John, who appears in various guises in the following pages and who, like the Velveteen Rabbit, is very Real. "And once you become Real," said the Skin Horse, "you can't become unreal again. It lasts for always."

ACKNOWLEDGMENTS

I'm deeply grateful to the following people for their help in making this book possible: Caroline McClurg for suggesting a sequel and for her steadfast support; Marion Crook for her insights and wisdom on adoption issues; my ever-growing circle of amazing writer friends who inspire me and who contributed so much to the writing of *Tangled Web*; and to Bob Tyrrell and Andrew Wooldridge of Orca Books for having faith in the story and for guiding me in the right direction.

....

The song lyrics on page 68 are by Will Smith, "Just the Two of Us"

....

"O what a tangled web we weave, when first we practice to deceive!"
– Sir Walter Scott
1771 - 1832

.... one

Tanner sucked hard on the straw, hoping to get one last sip of Coke from the plastic cup. No luck. He shook it, rattling the ice cubes in the bottom, and tried again. Still nothing. Pulling off the lid, he tipped the cup to his lips, but received only a mouthful of ice.

"Still thirsty?" asked his dad.

"No." Tanner pushed the cup away. "Just bored I guess." He glanced up at the TV monitor that announced the airline arrivals and departures and realized that only three minutes had passed since the last time he checked. He sighed. "I hate waiting."

"Me too," said his mom. "And the longer we wait, the more uncomfortable I feel about letting you go back to Vancouver."

"Oh Mom," groaned Tanner. "Let's not go over that again."

"I can't help it, honey. The last time you went there you were abducted by a drug-trafficking criminal and nearly killed."

"Like that's going to happen twice, Mom? I don't think so. Besides," Tanner said, "Hap's in jail. There's nothing to worry about."

"When you're a mother, Tanner, there's always something to worry about."

"I guess I'll never know about that," Tanner answered, grinning, but the word "mother" triggered another thought. For almost fifteen years he'd assumed that this woman was his biological mother, but when he was abducted last Christmas he had learned he was adopted and had an identical twin brother named Alex, who'd been raised by another family. At first Tanner was so excited about discovering he had a brother that he'd given the adoption very little thought, but lately he'd begun wondering about his biological parents — especially his mother. Why had she given up her twin boys and, even worse, allowed the social workers to separate them?

"Your attention please, Vancouver-bound passengers. Canadian flight 519 is now ready for boarding. Would all passengers please proceed to Gate 15."

Tanner jumped up. "Finally," he said. He grabbed his backpack and waited while his parents gathered their things. He noticed that his mother's eyes were already filling with tears and they weren't even at the security gate yet. He turned away. He wished he could just leave them here and get on with it. He hated these scenes. He'd miss them too, but he was only going away for two weeks — one week of hockey camp and one week of visiting Alex.

"Don't forget to phone every third day," reminded his dad for the umpteenth time as they walked through the Edmonton terminal toward the departure gate.

"I won't, Dad."

"And get those autographs from the pros that you promised your sister."

"I will."

Finally, to Tanner's relief, they arrived at the security check. "Anything else you want to remind me about?"

His father put his arm around Tanner's shoulder and pulled him close. "Have a good time, son, and work on that hockey."

"I will." He turned to his mother. "And you? Any final words of wisdom?"

Tears streamed down her face as she reached up to hug the son who towered above her. "Just stay out of trouble," she said.

"It's a promise." He gently pulled himself away from her embrace, walked toward the metal detector and dropped his bag on the conveyer belt. When the security guard gave the signal, he walked through the electronic gate himself. As he collected his bag on the other side he looked back at his parents, who were still standing there, each with an arm around the other. He smiled, waved, then turned to walk down the long corridor to the gate. He didn't look back again.

········

As the plane reached its cruising altitude and leveled off, Tanner leaned his head against the window and looked down. Below him the prairie spread out like a giant quilt, but he could see the peaks of the Rocky Mountains in the distance. Once again his thoughts traveled back to the last time he'd made this trip to the coast. It was amazing how much things could change in just six months. On that trip he had crossed the Rockies on a bus with his hockey team. He'd been a mess: a tired, irritable wreck. It was because of the nightmare, the one that had haunted his sleep every night. But, despite the horrendous headaches and losing his place on the first string, he'd gone on the road trip anyway because he needed to get to the coast. The nightmare was about swimming in salt water and he was sure that by going to the ocean he would understand the meaning of it.

He'd found out all right. But he had almost died in the process.

When he saw the flight attendants serving meals, Tanner put his seat back into the upright position, then lowered his table to accept a tray.

"You should see your face," laughed the young woman.

Tanner glanced up, unsure of what she'd read in his expression.

"A sandwich and a little bowl of fruit cocktail doesn't really fill up a young man, does it? I'll deliver the rest of these," she said, without waiting for an answer, "and see what else I can find. I have a nephew about your age," she added, "and I know it takes more than one fancy little sandwich to satisfy him." She hurried off.

Tanner watched her work her way up the aisle as he gulped down his lunch and then went back to staring out the window. It was as though she'd read his mind, he thought. Was it possible that he sent messages to other people too?

The sandwich had quelled some of the butterflies that were flapping around in his stomach, and his thoughts turned back to his brother. Finding a summer hockey camp in Vancouver had been Alex's ingenious work. It was just the excuse Tanner needed to get back to the city he'd been born in, to see his brother and to spend more time with him. He had been waiting for this trip for so long that he couldn't believe he was finally on his way.

Maybe he could let Alex know where he was right now. Tanner closed his eyes and focused on a mental image of the mountain range below him. He pushed the picture as hard as he could, then allowed his mind to go blank until a picture of a trophy popped into his head. That was the signal they'd developed to confirm that the transmission was successful, that they'd connected. Tanner smiled and was just about to open his eyes when another picture flashed through his mind, and then a whole series of pictures. He saw the Lions Gate Bridge, a body on a stretcher, a man striking a woman ...

"Are you okay?" asked the flight attendant. "You look like you want to kill someone."

Tanner looked up, startled. She had come up from behind him and was standing in the aisle holding a basket filled with small packages of nuts, cookies and crackers. He felt his cheeks get warm.

"Yeah. Sure." But was he? His heart was drumming inside his chest. What were those pictures all about?

"I brought some goodies to fill you up." She reached across the empty seats and handed him the basket. Their hands touched briefly, and he noticed how soft her skin was.

"Thanks," he mumbled, quickly forgetting about the weird images that he'd just seen. He wondered again whether she could read his thoughts — especially the ones he was having about her. He felt too awkward to make eye contact with her, so he stared at her perfectly manicured nails.

"No problem," she said. "Enjoy." She winked when he finally looked up, then hustled off.

Yes, he thought to himself, this trip is starting off a lot better than the last one. He opened a package of peanuts and glanced out the window, but just then the plane flew into a bank of clouds, blocking out the view and casting a gloomy shadow into the interior of the plane.

.... **two**

When the image of mountain peaks sprang into his head, Alex shut off the vacuum cleaner and glanced about. No one else from the airplane cleaning crew was in sight, so he sank into a seat and closed his eyes. He focused on the form of the trophy that sat on the bookshelf in his room at his uncle's house. He pushed the image and opened his eyes, but instead of returning to his work, he allowed his mind to wander back to another picture that had once popped into his head: a picture of the Lions Gate Bridge. That was the image that had led him to his brother in the first place, six months ago.

He felt weary just thinking about that incident. He sat back and closed his eyes again. Suddenly a flood of other images washed over him: his brother's brutalized body being carried away on a stretcher from where it was dumped under that bridge … the vicious expression on Hap's face as he smacked Maureen simply for having a conversation with him … the starkness of the homeless men's shelter he'd slept in when he'd escaped from Hap.

The images began to come faster, and all jumbled up. His

father's arm, raised and ready to strike him ... Tanner on the crisp white hospital sheets, his face swollen and bruised beyond recognition ... the faces of the beggars he'd met when he was practically living on the streets of Vancouver ...

"Nappin' on the job?"

Alex's eyes flew open. Jim, his crew supervisor, stood looking down at him.

"I'm sorry, sir. I don't know what came over me." He sat up. "I felt so dizzy all of a sudden." He flexed his cramped hands. They'd been gripping his knees so tightly that they'd stiffened up.

"Are you okay?"

"Yeah, I am now."

"Good, 'cause it's almost 12:30. Didn't you say that's when your brother's plane is landing?"

Alex jumped to his feet. He couldn't be late meeting Tanner. "Yeah. Thanks."

"You're sure you're okay?"

"Yeah, really."

"Then we'll forget about this little incident." He slapped Alex's back. "You've already proved to be a much harder worker than most of the summer relief I get. Your uncle was right about you," he added. "It's a nice change, because most kids who get jobs through their connections are lazy bums."

Alex's foot began to tap. Once this man got started ...

"But, like I said, you've worked out fine." Jim checked his watch again. "You'd better run now. Have a nice lunch."

Alex jogged through a long maze of twisting corridors that led him to the Arrivals terminal. He wiped the sweat off his brow with his sleeve and glanced up at a computer monitor hanging from the ceiling. The plane had already landed. He searched the crowd and started slightly when he saw Tanner waiting by the luggage carousel at the gate. He still wasn't used to seeing his double. If you had grown up with your twin, he thought, you'd be accustomed to it, but finding out you have a double after fourteen years is something else.

"Tanner!" he called. "Over here!"

Tanner waved and sauntered over to where Alex was standing. There was a waist-high barrier that separated the arriving passengers from the friends and relatives who were there to greet them. They reached out simultaneously and did a high-five in the air.

"Nice coveralls, " Tanner commented, checking out his brother's work clothes. "If you're a grease monkey," he added, emphatically.

Alex grinned and did a clumsy pirouette. He tugged on the badge attached to his chest. "Quite the hottie, eh?"

Tanner peered at the photo ID that Alex held out. It could be a picture of either of them.

"Hey, maybe you could take a few shifts for me," Alex suggested. "No one would know the difference."

"Depends on how much you get paid."

"I'll pay you two bucks an hour."

"Get lost." Tanner reached across the barrier to punch his brother in the arm, but Alex stepped back and pointed in the opposite direction.

"Your luggage is coming."

Tanner glanced back, realized it was a bluff, but it was too late. Alex had snatched the Edmonton Oilers cap off his head.

"Hey!" Tanner reached over the barrier once more, but Alex simply stepped back again. "You just wait," Tanner said, "There's nothing like revenge."

A minute later the suitcases really did begin to slide down the ramp and before long Tanner joined Alex on the other side of the barrier with a bulky hockey bag, a hockey stick and a suitcase.

"My uncle's not picking you up until 1:30," Alex said, glancing at his watch. "You want to get lunch at the cafeteria?"

"I had some," Tanner replied, "but I'll grab a drink while you eat."

They found a table beside a window with a good view of the busy tarmac and the runways. Once again Alex felt charged up, exhilarated by being so close to the activity of the airport. Hearing the engines kick into life and then watching the plane roll into position for takeoff was a rush, but it was nothing like watching it actually thunder down the runway, then lift up, airborne and graceful. Following the path of an incoming plane was just as exciting. Once he caught sight of the silver dot in the distance his eyes never wavered until it had safely touched down and he could hear the reverse thrusters roar into action.

"I got your message," he said, popping a French fry into his mouth. "It was different seeing the Rockies from above. When I went to Edmonton at spring break I could barely see the peaks from the bus window."

"Maybe next time you come to see me you can fly," Tanner said. "Now that you've got a job."

"Yeah. Mom's working too, so things are better."

Tanner nodded, but Alex noticed that at the mention of the word "mom", his brother's eyes had glazed over and he seemed to retreat into a world of his own. They sat in comfortable silence for awhile, Alex mesmerized by the steady stream of aircraft traffic, while Tanner remained lost in thought. Finally Alex spoke again.

"Did I tell you I was able to get the week after next off, the week after your hockey camp?"

"Sweet." Tanner's eyes cleared.

"We can do anything you'd like. Hang out at the beach, hike, rent some kayaks and go paddling...whatever."

"Perfect," Tanner said, but Alex sensed he wasn't referring

to the list of options he'd just rattled off. He studied his brother, tried to tap into his thoughts, but with no results. For most of the week of spring break that Alex had spent in Edmonton, they had explored the dimensions of their telepathic connection. Reading each other's thoughts was not something they were very successful at.

"What do you mean by 'sweet'?" Alex asked.

Tanner studied his brother. "I've got a plan." He glanced at his watch. "But there's no time to fill you in now. We'll talk tonight."

Alex was intrigued. He and Tanner had kept in constant communication since the day they'd met at the end of December, and it wasn't like Tanner to keep any secrets. They'd bonded instantly and both felt they had fourteen years of catching up to do. When the cost of their long-distance phone bills skyrocketed they began to send off e-mail messages to each other almost daily. And, just like Tanner had done earlier, they were able to send mental images, if not thoughts, telepathically.

Alex checked his watch too. "I guess you're right. It'll have to wait. I'll walk you out to the loading zone where my uncle's picking you up."

Tanner handed Alex his hockey bag and gathered up the rest of his things. He led the way to the door of the cafeteria. "Which way?"

Alex hesitated, looking around.

"What's up? You work here. Don't you know your way around?"

"I'm just trying to decide which route to take." He lowered his voice. "I don't like going by the lockers and car rentals. That's where Hap used to do his drug deals. It gives me the creeps." He turned left. "We'll take the elevator."

As they walked through the airport together, Alex was aware of the curious looks they were getting from complete strangers. He glanced at his brother. It was like looking in a mirror. He wondered if he'd ever get used to being a twin. As they approached the wide doors that led outside, he checked their reflections in the glass. Even their gaits were identical.

Alex looked briefly at the idling cars that sat in the loading zone. "I guess we beat him."

Tanner nodded, and they moved back into the shade near the doors. "It's a lot hotter than the last time I was here."

"Yeah, I guess," Alex said, thinking back to the cool, gray day that he'd led Officer Russell to Tanner's body in West Vancouver.

Tanner leaned against the wall, arms folded across his chest. "So? Why was I getting all that weird feedback on the plane?"

"What weird feedback?"

"I was seeing Hap's face, and the Lions Gate Bridge, and myself..."

"Oh, that feedback. Sorry. I didn't know I was sending it. After I sent you the trophy I began thinking back on everything ... I guess I just kept sending stuff."

"That's a first."

"Yeah." Alex looked down at his hands, remembering how white his knuckles had turned.

"So, do you think we should hang out in Stanley Park next week?"

"Very funny."

"It was weird, though, wasn't it," Tanner reminisced, watching a car pull away from the curb, "that you escaped from Hap in Stanley Park the day before I went there with Cara. If I hadn't gone there, Hap wouldn't have kidnapped me by mistake and you and I would never have met."

"I know. Fluky or what? I wonder if he would've tracked me down eventually." A chill ran down Alex's spine despite the heat.

Tanner shrugged. "And if you hadn't heard about me on the news ... "

"I know. I would never have known that he'd abducted the wrong kid, and then I wouldn't have twigged in when I picked up the picture of the Lions Gate Bridge in my head and then ... man, I hate to even think." Alex paused, then continued. "You were a mess. Hap kicked the crap out of you."

"Yeah, but I'm tough." Tanner stood up straighter. "I handled it. Now, had it been you ... you'd be a goner," he teased.

Alex's uncle pulled up to the curb before Alex had a chance to defend himself. Mr. Bradshaw hopped out of his car and rushed around to shake Tanner's hand.

"You're looking good, Tanner. Last time I saw you ..."

"Yeah, we were just talking about that. I wasn't a pretty sight, was I?"

"No." Mr. Bradshaw studied him for a moment. "Anyway," he continued, opening the trunk of the car, "it's great to have you here. It looks like you're all ready to play hockey on Monday. Mind if I watch? It's been a long time since my own sons played."

"That'd be great, Mr. Bradshaw."

"Please, Tanner, call me John, or Uncle John. I really am your uncle, in a way, right? If I'm Alex's uncle and he's your twin brother, that makes me your uncle too." He studied Tanner, eyebrows raised expectantly.

"Yeah, I guess it does, sort of," Tanner agreed. "It gets kind of complicated, doesn't it?"

"Only if we make it complicated. Now hop in. I'm sure Alex has to get back to work and besides, this is only a five-minute loading zone."

Alex watched his uncle's car pull away and then jogged back through the tangle of corridors that led him to the plane he'd been cleaning before lunch. As he picked up his vacuum and began pushing it back and forth he thought about his uncle's theory. If his Uncle John was Tanner's uncle, wouldn't his mom become Tanner's mom too, and vice versa? They'd each have two moms. He smiled as he thought of it. The same would be true of their dads. The smile disappeared. He could think of Tanner's dad as his own, but he certainly wouldn't want to subject Tanner to his father. God forbid. In fact, Alex's mom was filing for divorce, and Alex wished he could also sever the ties. Permanently.

No, Tanner was better off with just one father in his life. His own.

three

John Bradshaw explained his theory to Alex's mom, Pat, at dinner that night. "So, by extension," he concluded, "that would mean that you now have two sons where you used to have only one."

Tanner watched Mrs. Swanson's reaction. She smiled at him, a smile that made her gentle blue eyes shine, perhaps too brightly. Were those tears he saw welling up in them?

"That's nice," she said, her voice quivering. Then she lowered her eyes and retreated back into her private world. It was as if someone had turned out the lights.

Tanner was puzzled. He didn't know what reaction he'd expected, but it was certainly more than that one. He shoveled a huge forkful of mashed potatoes into his mouth while he mulled it over. In some ways she seemed like the perfect mom, so kind and patient, but perhaps years of abuse had made her sad and introverted. Having her son accidentally discover that he was adopted and had an identical twin brother would be weird. He cut a chunk of sausage and smothered it in hot mustard. And now, here he was, the twin, sitting at the same table.

As he understood it, she'd always wanted to tell Alex that he was adopted but her husband wouldn't allow it. Last winter, after the truth of their separation and adoption had been revealed, Alex had said, "Now I know why my dad hates me. He always wanted his own kids but adoption was his only choice. He must have been pissed off that I wasn't his real kid."

Tanner shuddered. It was just a lucky break for him that he hadn't been given to the Swansons at the time of the adoption. It was like the flip of a coin. It could so easily have been him that had gone to Alex's parents and Alex to his.

"Would you boys do the dishes?" asked Alex's uncle, glancing at the wall clock. "There's a movie playing that Pat and I want to see, but we need to hurry to get there in time." He carried his plate to the counter. "Unless you'd like to join us," he added. "You're more than welcome, of course."

Tanner looked at Alex, and they shook their heads in unison. This was perfect, Tanner thought. With the adults gone, he could present Alex with his plan and not be worried about them overhearing anything.

"Thanks anyway, Uncle John," Alex said. "I think we'd just like to hang out tonight."

"That's what we figured," he answered. "We'll see you later then."

As she followed her brother out the door, Pat Swanson slid her hand into the mailbox, checking for flyers. "Oh look, Alex," she said. "A letter for you." She paused. "That's odd," she continued. "This is Saturday, and I thought I'd already brought in yesterday's mail."

"You must have thought wrong, Mom." Alex took the envelope and gently guided her back out the door, but before he could even glance at the handwriting, Tanner snatched it from him and threw it on the desk that sat in the corner of the kitchen.

"Hey!"

"You can read it later." Tanner wasn't going to wait while Alex opened his mail or until they'd finished the dishes to un-veil his scheme. He pushed Alex into a chair as soon as he heard the car back out of the driveway. "I've got a plan."

"So you mentioned. Spit it out."

"We're going to search for our biological mother."

"For who?"

"You heard me. Our biological mother. You know, our birth mother. The lady who had us." Tanner studied Alex's face, try-ing to read his reaction. But Alex just sat there, staring at him. "Well aren't you just a bit curious about her? Don't you want to know why we were given up for adoption?"

"Yeah, I guess ..."

"We might even have other brothers or sisters. Who knows? Maybe our mom is trying to find us ... to see what we're like, or even if we're alive."

"She's not really our mom, Tanner. She just gave birth to us."

"You know what I mean." Tanner studied Alex, puzzled. "What's wrong?"

Alex hesitated, as if choosing his words carefully. "You've got a great family already, Tanner. Do you really want to mess that up?"

"I won't be messing anything up — I need to know who she is. After all, she *was* our mother for nine months. We *are* her flesh and blood. I look in the mirror every morning and won-der if I look like her. Or do I look like my biological father? Which one of them did I get this stupid little piece of hair from, this one that always sticks straight up at the back?" He ran his hand over his head and, finding the wayward hairs, tried to press them down. "You've got the same thing." He watched as Alex's hand inadvertently mirrored his own, attempting to flat-ten an identical tuft. "And sometimes when I'm walking down the street and I see someone who looks like me I wonder if we could be related. Maybe I've even met our birth mom and I don't know it!" He paused, reflecting on what he'd said. "I'm sure my mom and dad will understand why I have to do this. They'll probably even help me. It doesn't change how I feel about them."

"Right. This is the same mom and dad that didn't even tell you that you'd been adopted?"

"There was a good explanation for that. They said they always meant to, but the time never seemed just right, and then they waited too long and decided there was no point. They're really sorry about it. In fact, I could use that as part of my argument. I could tell them that if I'd always known I was adopted it would be easier to accept, but finding out about it at fourteen was such a shock that I need to learn more."

"I don't know, Tanner." Alex shook his head.

"What's not to know, Alex? I'm not suggesting we leave our families or anything."

"Did you ever think about it from her point of view? Our birth mother's? She put us up for adoption. She didn't want to raise us then, so there's a good chance she won't want to see us now."

"Fine. If that happens, we let it go. But at least we give her the chance — let her explain why she didn't keep us."

"That's pretty obvious, don't you think?"

"What do you mean?"

"She probably got knocked up by some guy who wouldn't marry her. She was smart to put us up for adoption. Can you imagine raising twins if you're a single mom?"

"You don't know that happened."

"It's a good guess."

"Well, I'd like to know for sure."

Alex laughed. "What if you find her and discover she's a

total idiot? How will you feel then?"

Tanner remained serious. "Maybe she's a famous celebrity. Either way, she owes us an explanation."

"What explanation?"

"Why she gave us up. Who our father is." Tanner saw Alex sit up and hoped that this was the hook he'd been looking for. "Maybe she ended up marrying our father after all. You never know, we might end up finding our biological father at the same time."

"You mean the sperm donor?"

"Don't be so negative, Alex. We don't know the circumstances. Maybe he wanted her to keep us but someone else forced her to put us up for adoption." He paused, studying Alex's face. "Maybe he'd even want to be a father to you when he heard your adoptive father's a jerk."

"I didn't know you had such a vivid imagination."

"Yeah? Well I didn't know you were such a wuss."

They sat in silence for awhile.

"Do you remember Katie, my golden retriever?" Tanner decided to take a new approach.

"Yeah. Why?"

"Remember I told you she had a litter of puppies a couple months ago?"

"Yeah. So?"

"Well, I watched the whole birth thing. It was pretty gross seeing her lick the blood off them and all that, but it was also kinda awesome. And she knew just how to look after them. Who taught her?"

Alex ignored the rhetorical question.

"And protective? Whoa! She wouldn't even let my mom go near them at first, and she worships Mom." Tanner leaned closer to Alex, his eyes narrowed. "That's the first time I really got it, you know, that stuff about instinct, and it blew me away.

Katie became a wreck looking after those puppies."

Alex drummed his fingers on the table. "That's all very interesting, Tanner, but what's your dog got to do with anything?"

"I can't stop thinking about the bond that happened between her and her puppies." Tanner studied his brother, wondering if he grasped what he was trying to say, but Alex just slumped back in his chair, folded his arms across his chest and stared out the window.

Tanner continued, his voice raised in pitch. "Bond is not a strong enough word to describe it, either. It's more like ..." Tanner paused, trying to think of an example his brother would understand. "It's more like what you and I have — our connection — and you know what that's like." He glared at his brother's blank expression. "Think about it, Alex." His voice was choked with emotion. "If that bond is there between a dog and her puppies, imagine what it's like for a human mother and her baby — or in our case, babies!" Tanner banged the table with his fist to stress his point but Alex sat mute, seemingly unmoved by this passionate plea. A Rockwell collector's plate, depicting a happy family scene, vibrated slightly where it hung on the far wall. Tanner glanced at it and knew he was getting too worked up.

He leaned farther forward and continued in a soft but insistent voice, "I just know in my heart that she didn't want to give us up, Alex, and that she's probably as anxious to meet us as I am to meet her." He swallowed hard, trying to calm himself, but it was too late. The decorative plate fell to the floor and shattered. For a long moment both boys stared at the mess. They knew exactly what had happened.

"Well?" he asked Alex, suddenly feeling exhausted. "Will you think about it?"

Alex took a deep breath and let it out slowly. He got up,

and while handing Tanner a broom he'd pulled out of a corner closet, he answered, "I guess."

Tanner jumped up. "Yes!" Pretending the broom was a hockey stick, he whooped and rode it around the kitchen the way he'd ride it around the hockey rink after scoring a goal.

Alex couldn't help laughing. "I said I'd think about it. That's not the same as a yes."

"Close enough." Tanner snatched the Edmonton Oilers cap off Alex's head and slapped it back on his own. "We better get to work." He glanced at the pieces of plate on the floor. "Do you think they'll notice one is missing?"

"Not if we don't point it out to them." Alex studied the wall that was covered in plates. "We just have to rearrange them so there's no gaping hole in the collection." Carefully avoiding the shards of china on the floor, he lifted the last plate in the row off its hook and hung it where the broken one had once been. Then he pulled the extra hook out of the wall. "There, good as new. Now sweep up the mess while I start the dishes."

As Alex walked by the desk on his way to the sink he noticed the envelope that still lay there, unopened. He picked it up and turned it over.

"Who's it from?" Tanner asked, glancing at him.

Alex looked puzzled. "There's no return address. I don't recognize the handwriting either." He ripped it open, pulled out the single sheet of paper and dropped the envelope back onto the desk. Then he unfolded the sheet of paper.

Tanner continued to sweep up the broken plate. Suddenly he sensed how still Alex was standing. "Is something the matter?" he asked.

Alex didn't say anything. He just handed him the letter.

.... four

Alex watched while Tanner read the single sentence on the sheet of paper.

"I know where you live?" Tanner looked at his brother. "What's that supposed to mean?"

Alex shrugged. He tried to fight the panic that was chewing its way through his stomach and up to his throat. "Probably just my dad."

"That doesn't make sense. He knows that *you know* he knows where you're living."

Alex laughed nervously. "Well, you know my dad. When he's drinking he says and does a lot of things he doesn't mean. He probably wrote that right before he passed out dead drunk."

Tanner put down the piece of paper and began to load the dishwasher. They worked in silence for a few minutes.

"Is that his handwriting?"

Alex swallowed hard. "No."

"Then who do you really think wrote it?"

"Probably a chick from school. They all have the hots for me." Alex laughed again, hoping his voice concealed his fear.

"Very funny, Alex."

"Glad you think so."

Tanner pulled the plug from the bottom of the sink and wiped the table. Alex put away the last few dishes.

"What do you want to do now?" Alex asked his brother, refusing to discuss the letter any further.

Tanner shrugged. "Wanna watch the tube for awhile?"

Alex nodded. "Sure, I'm always bagged after work anyway." He picked up the letter, folded it and stuffed it in his back pocket as he followed Tanner down the hall to the den.

Alex stared at the flickering screen, but his thoughts were miles away. He knew Tanner didn't buy his stupid story that the letter came from a girl, but neither of them could bring themselves to discuss other possibilities...

Alex thought back to the time shortly after he'd led the police to Tanner's brutalized body. He tried to remember the conversation he'd had with Officer Russell.

"A witness has stepped forward with enough evidence against Hap to warrant an arrest," he'd said. Alex knew who the witness was. It was Maureen, the young woman who had found him when he was penniless and desperate and had introduced him to Hap, the drug dealer. She'd thought she was helping him and had assumed that he'd work for Hap. She was dead wrong, of course, but her heart was in the right place and when things got really ugly she'd gone to the police and told them all about Hap's criminal activity.

So he knew for sure that Hap had been arrested. Had he sent him the letter from jail or had he told one of his buddies to send it? What had Maureen said? "He has eyes everywhere." Did he still have eyes everywhere, even while he was behind bars?

What if he wasn't in jail? What if he had a really good lawyer who'd managed to get him off on some technicality?

Alex jumped up and went to the bathroom. He turned on the cold water and splashed his face with it, trying to cool the burning flush that had suddenly come over him. He dried his face, flipped down the lid of the toilet and sat on it. He looked at his hands. They were trembling slightly.

Stay calm, he told himself. You don't know anything yet. Tomorrow he'd phone Officer Russell and ask him what had become of Hap. Then, if Hap wasn't in jail, he'd tell him about the letter. He wouldn't talk to Tanner about this. There was no point in both of them worrying.

Alex jumped when there was a loud bang on the bathroom door. "What are you doing in there?" Tanner demanded.

"I'll be right out." He took a deep breath. With a plan of action in place he felt better. Officer Russell would know what to do. He checked his hands. The trembling had stopped. He flushed the toilet, ran the water again and opened the bathroom door.

Tanner was in the hall, waiting impatiently. "'Bout time," he said, pushing his way past Alex and banging the door shut behind him.

....

Later, as he lay in bed, Alex thought of the plate that had fallen from the kitchen wall that evening. "Have you been breaking a lot of stuff lately?" he asked his brother, who was lying on a cot on the other side of the room.

"No. Only when I'm really ticked off. I can *will* it to happen but it creeps me out. I'd rather just forget about it."

"Yeah, I know what you mean. I did some research on the Net about telepathy and all that stuff."

"Yeah? So did I. What did you find out?"

"That being able to send pictures to each other is pretty weird. We're freaks."

"No," Alex corrected him. "We're gifted."

"Call it what you want. But I also found out that making stuff move like we do is called telekinesis. They say it mostly happens to stressed-out kids. Somehow your energy leaves your body in a kind of vibration and when it hits something, it moves it, or in my case, usually knocks something over and breaks it, like that plate tonight."

"That's about it, all right."

" I find that if I *will* it to happen I'm completely wiped afterwards."

Alex nodded. "Yeah, me too. Probably because of the strong feelings that you have to muster up to make it happen. Anytime your adrenaline gets pumping that hard, you're left feeling drained. Or I am, anyway."

"Yeah, you're probably right."

The room was quiet for a few minutes. Alex thought Tanner must have fallen asleep so was startled when the question came.

"Have you thought anymore about doing the search, Alex?"

"Give me a break, Tanner. It's only been a couple of hours."

"I know, but for me it was an instantaneous decision. As soon as I thought of it I knew I had to do it."

Alex sighed. "So you mean you're going to do it anyway, with or without my help?"

"Yeah. I have to."

Alex sighed again and rolled over onto his side, suddenly feeling exhausted. "Then I guess I have to, too."

"Yes!" Tanner was up, pummeling Alex with his pillow. "Yes! Yes! Yes! I knew you'd see the light. Thanks, Alex. You won't regret it." He kept hitting his brother with the pillow.

"I already do." He blocked the pillow as best as he could but he suddenly felt so tired that he couldn't bring himself to swing his own pillow.

Tanner gave up the attack when he got no resistance and settled back onto his cot.

Alex was just about asleep when a thought occurred to him. "Don't say anything to my mom about this yet. I need to run it past her ... gently. I don't think she's gonna like it."

"Me neither. But your uncle's cool."

"Yeah, he is."

"And retired, so he's got time. He'll probably help us."

"Maybe." Alex could hear Tanner's excitement build again, but he'd heard enough of his brother's crazy ideas for one day so he quickly brought it to a close. "Good night, Tanner. I'm beat."

"Good night." Alex heard his brother flip over onto his side, but he knew Tanner wouldn't fall asleep quickly. No, he'd lie in the dark mapping out his strategy. Alex wondered what made them so different. If they'd been raised in the same home, with the same parents, would they be more alike?

Assuming he'd never know for sure, he drifted off to sleep.

.... five

As he climbed the hill he felt the warm sun on his skin and he breathed deeply. He was moving forward easily, without strain. But wait. He felt a presence behind him. Should he turn around and face it? He didn't want to. Life was good and if he faced it he felt the world might come crashing down around him. He tried to ignore the presence and keep moving forward, but the good feelings of the day were gone. A strong headwind had come up and blocked his progress. He could barely move now. Grabbing a branch for support, he braced himself, then turned around to see what was behind him. It was a woman and she was trying to tell him something. He could see her lips moving, her eyes pleading with him, but he couldn't make out the words. The wind was carrying them away. He turned away from her, determined to confront the wind and keep walking, but a crowd had gathered at the top of the hill. They were studying him carefully, watching to see which way he would go. He couldn't move forward but he also couldn't go back — she was there. He had to get away, back to the good feelings, but it was getting hard to breathe. He tried to draw a deep breath but nothing happened. He tried to shout at the crowd, tell them to go away, but without breathing he couldn't speak, let alone shout. He sat down and put his head between his legs, struggling for air. He thumped his chest, tried coughing. How could he still be alive if he wasn't breathing? He was going to die and those people just stood there staring at him. Once again he tried to scream at them, tell them to help him, he was suffocating ...

....

"Tanner. Wake up, dear. You're having a nightmare."

He opened his eyes. Alex's mom was bending over him, gently shaking his shoulder. He heard the click as Alex turned on the reading light on the wall beside his bed. Alex's uncle was standing in the doorway.

"Oh no. Not again." He buried his head in his pillow. He must have made a huge commotion to wake everyone up. "I'm sorry."

Another nightmare. He thought he was finished with all that. Then he felt the familiar throb in his head. He sat up and glared at his brother. Somehow he was picking up Alex's worries in his dreams again. He was about to blast him, but Alex shook his head ever so slightly. *Not now,* his eyes pleaded.

"Can I get you something?" asked Alex's uncle.

"No, I'm okay. I'm afraid I'm known for my noisy nightmares. I must be anxious about the hockey camp."

"Yes, that's probably it," murmured Mrs. Swanson, joining her brother in the doorway. "If there's nothing we can get you then we'll go back to bed."

"I'm fine. Sorry I woke you. I'll try not to let it happen again," he added, realizing the futility of the statement as he said it. He watched as the door shut behind them before he turned on his brother. "Okay, what's going on?"

"I can't keep any secrets, can I?"

"'Fraid not. It's the letter, isn't it." A statement, not a question.

"Yeah." Alex flicked off the reading light.

It took Tanner a moment to make out his brother's shape in the dark room. "You think it's Hap, don't you?"

"Uh-huh."

"Me too. But he's in jail, isn't he?"

"Well, I assumed he was because he was arrested."

Tanner stared at his brother's silhouette. "You mean you don't know for sure?"

"He was arrested after Maureen blew the whistle on him. Wouldn't *you* assume he was in jail?"

"Alex! You can't assume anything. What are we going to do?"

"I'm going to phone Officer Russell tomorrow. He'll tell me what's going on."

"Are you going to tell him about the letter?"

"Yeah. Don't you think I should?"

"Yeah, I do." Tanner had laid his head back on the pillow. "You're just going to phone him though, not go to the station, right?"

"Yeah, why?"

"Just wondering." But that wasn't true. It occurred to him that if it was Hap who had sent the letter, he might be watching the house, possibly following them. They shouldn't be seen going to the police. On the other hand, he didn't want to worry Alex any more than necessary. The more disturbed Alex felt, the more likely Tanner would have nightmares. "It's probably nothing. Officer Russell would have warned you if Hap wasn't in jail."

"That's true."

Tanner could hear by the tone in Alex's voice that he was comforted by that thought. He yawned. "Let's go back to sleep."

Alex's bed creaked as he rolled onto his side. Before long,

Tanner could hear his brother's breathing change to the slow, deep rhythm of sleep. He turned his attention back to the letter. If it was from Hap, why a letter? Did the creep just want to intimidate Alex?

Tanner had watched Alex shove the note into his pocket and throw the envelope into a bin under the sink. Perhaps they should keep that envelope. Officer Russell might want to see it.

He rolled off the cot, quietly opened the bedroom door and crept down the hall to the kitchen. He flicked on the light and opened the cupboard under the sink where the recycling bins were stored. Mr. Bradshaw was fastidious about his recycling. The envelope was right there on the top of the scrap-paper bin. Tanner pulled it out and studied it. Something was wrong, but what? He yawned. He was too tired to figure it out tonight. He shut off the light and went back to the room he shared with Alex. He flopped onto his cot and closed his eyes. He was almost asleep when it hit him.

The envelope wasn't postmarked.

....

It was a relief to wake up Sunday morning feeling refreshed. There had been no more nightmares. The last thing Tanner needed before hockey camp was to be sleep deprived again. The lack of sleep, caused by the nightmares, had practically destroyed his game last winter. He had Alex to thank for that.

Tanner studied his brother. He looked so young and untroubled in his sleep. Why, he wondered, didn't Alex pick up his distress signals during sleep the way he picked up Alex's? If he had, he certainly would have had nightmares last night after Tanner discovered that the letter hadn't been delivered by a letter carrier. The implications of that were disturbing. Alex was the lucky one, he thought. He only had to live with his own worries at night. He didn't have to share Tanner's like Tanner shared his.

"I thought you were going to sleep all day," Tanner said when Alex finally opened his eyes.

"Yeah, well, I work hard, I get tired."

"Work? You call what you do work?"

"Yeah, I do. You wouldn't last a day."

"Get real." They went to the kitchen, where Alex poached eggs and made toast and hash browns while Tanner created a "power" shake with ingredients he found in the fridge. Alex's mom and uncle peered over the top of their Sunday newspaper, watched the boys cooking, and suddenly decided to go to church and have brunch on their way home.

"We only have two weeks," Tanner said when they were alone. He smothered his eggs in ketchup. "And the first week is mostly a write-off because I'm at hockey camp and you're working, so we'd better get started on our search today."

"Whatever you say." Alex took a big swig of Tanner's power shake, froze, then leapt to his feet and spat it into the sink. "What did you put in that?" he wailed.

"Just the usual kinda stuff — milk, eggs, wheat germ …"

"Eggs? Raw? Wheat *germ?*"

"Yeah."

"Oh gross."

Tanner ignored his brother. "Let's start with you phoning Officer Russell and we'll get that sorted out. I don't need a week of nightmares." He guzzled his shake. "Then we'll go down to the library and see if we can find any books on doing a search."

"Fine." Alex poured the remainder of his shake down the sink. "You do the dishes and I'll make the call."

"Oh yeah, that's fair."

"I thought so." Alex pulled the phone book out of the kitchen desk. Tanner grumbled but loaded the dishwasher anyway. He listened while Alex dialed the number and asked for Officer Russell. A moment later he watched his brother hang up the phone.

"Well?"

"He's not in today."

"Great. Isn't there anyone else you could talk to?"

Alex shrugged. "I guess, but I trust Officer Russell. I don't think I would have been able to convince anyone else to drive me to that spot under the Lions Gate Bridge where we found you last winter. But he trusted my hunch."

"Hunch? You call it a hunch?"

"You know what I mean. It's a hunch for lack of a better word."

Tanner wasn't convinced. "Anyone could tell you if Hap was in jail or not."

"But they wouldn't help us out if he's not in jail."

"Alex, we have to know."

"Fine." He sighed. "Then we'll go downtown and stop in at the police station. That way we can go to the main branch of the library. There'll be more books there anyhow."

Tanner frowned, still sensing that they shouldn't be seen going to the police. "Never mind. We'll go to a local library. Just remember to call him first thing in the morning."

"Okay. Let's get going then."

A few minutes later the boys were dressed and Alex's chores were done. He wrote a note telling his mom that they'd just gone for a walk and that they'd check in later.

On the way out the door Tanner noticed the mailbox. On impulse, he lifted the lid and peered in.

"There's no mail delivery on Sundays, dummy," said Alex, brushing past his brother and jogging down the steps.

But he was wrong. Tanner's heart skipped a beat when he saw the envelope in the mailbox. For a split second he considered just leaving it and not telling Alex, but then decided it would be wiser to know what it was. He pulled it out and read the handwriting. It was for Alex again, and this time there was no effort to disguise the fact that it had not come through the mail system.

Alex was waiting at the bottom of the stairs, watching his brother. "What is it?"

"It's another letter for you."

"Oh." He slowly walked back up the steps and took the letter from Tanner. "This one was hand delivered."

"So was the last one."

Alex raised his eyebrows, studied Tanner, then glanced up and down the quiet street. "Let's go back inside."

Tanner followed him into the kitchen and watched while he pulled two sheets of paper out of the envelope. He was sure he could see the color drain from Alex's face as he read them. Alex handed the pages to him and then slumped into a kitchen chair. Tanner glanced at the first sheet. There were only three words typed onto the center of the page. *You owe me*. The other slip of paper was a receipt from a clothing store. The purchase was for a leather coat valued at $300.00

Tanner held up the receipt. "What's this?"

Alex told the story in a monotone voice, staring at his hands the whole time. "The night I met Hap he took me to his house and I spent the night there. The next morning he assumed I had agreed to work for him even though I still didn't know what he did. He wouldn't take me back to my room downtown where my clothes were but insisted on buying me all new stuff." He looked up and pointed at the receipt that Tanner was still holding out. "That was for my leather coat."

"Where's the coat now?"

"Mom gave it to charity. We gave them the cowboy boots and everything else he bought me too."

Tanner stared at his brother. "What are we going to do?"

"Maybe I'll leave a note for him, saying I have a job now and will pay him back."

"I don't think you should make any kind of a deal with him. Wait until we've talked to Officer Russell."

"I think I'll call the police station again and leave a message for him to phone me as soon as he can."

"But then he'll call you here tomorrow when you're at work. Your mom might get the message. Are you planning to tell her about this?"

"No way. She'd freak."

They sat in silence for awhile.

"Maybe I'll call the police station and ask for his home phone number."

Tanner shook his head. "They'd never give it to you. You could be an ex-con with a grudge."

Alex sat up. "Then I'll ask if they can contact him at home and give him my number with a message to call me here, today, if he can."

"Your mom and Uncle John will be home soon."

"Then we'll have to make sure we answer the phone, won't we? And I'll also tell them that if he can't reach me here, today, he should contact me at work tomorrow."

"It's worth a try."

Alex got the phone book out again and made the call.

"What'd they say?" Tanner asked as soon as Alex hung up.

"We're in luck. The clerk remembered our case and thought Officer Russell wouldn't mind being contacted at home about it. She said she'd call him right away."

For the second time that morning, Tanner heaved a sigh of relief. He felt better already.

The call came twenty minutes later and, just as Alex had hoped, Officer Russell was extremely interested when Alex told him about the letters. Alex asked if he would meet them at a nearby coffee shop so they could talk. Officer Russell agreed and suggested they meet in two hours' time, so that he could go to the police station first and review the files on the case.

The boys got there early and chose a corner table where they would have some privacy. Alex watched the parking lot for the officer's arrival, and when he spotted him he jumped up to meet him at the door.

"Thanks for coming, sir, especially on your day off."

"No problem, Alex. I'm glad you called."

Alex led him to the table where Tanner was waiting. Tanner stood up and gripped the officer's outstretched hand.

"You're looking a lot more like your brother now than you did when I met you in the hospital, Tanner," the officer said.

Tanner smiled. "I'll take that as a compliment, I guess."

As they sat down the officer turned back to Alex. "I still can't get over the way you led me to him, Alex." He shook his head. "I see a lot of bizarre things in my line of work, but that takes the cake."

"Yeah, well, it came as kind of a surprise to me too." He sat quietly for a moment, thinking about the weird events of that day, six months earlier.

Officer Russell pulled a small phone out of his shirt pocket, flipped open the cover to check that the power was on and then snapped it shut. "Let's get something to eat and then we can talk," he said, returning the phone to his pocket. "The dough-nuts are on me." He pushed back his chair and led the way to the counter.

A few minutes later, with a variety pack full of doughnuts on the table in front of them, Alex decided to get directly to the point of the meeting. "Hap *is* in jail, isn't he?"

The officer glanced sharply at Alex, startled. "No, he's not, Alex. He's out on bail. You didn't know that?"

Alex slammed down his glass. "How can that be? You ar-rested him and Maureen has all the evidence you need."

"Yes, that's true, but someone was able to put up a bond for his bail, so he's out until his trial." He looked puzzled. "I don't know why you weren't informed." He shook his head and frowned. "Damn cutbacks. There have been more screw-ups at the station lately..."

"He hasn't even been tried yet?"

Officer Russell sighed. "No, he hasn't. It's crazy. Right now trial dates are being set for up to fourteen months after a charge is laid." He accepted a refill of coffee from a passing waitress. "We're lucky to have this trial slated for September," he added, pouring cream into his mug. "Before I came here, I went through the file to find out what's been happening in the in-vestigation, but I couldn't find much, so I placed a call to the chief investigator. He should be calling me any minute."

"Why aren't *you* the chief investigator?" asked Alex. "You

were the one involved in the beginning."

"This case is being handled by the serious crimes unit. I'm on general duty."

The phone bleeped. "That'll be him," the officer said. "Good timing." As he pulled out his phone he excused himself, pushed back his chair and walked away from the table.

Alex glanced at Tanner, who just shrugged as he shoved half of a jelly-filled doughnut into his mouth. Alex turned and studied the officer, who was standing near the door. He was doing a lot of listening but very little talking. A frown was etched deep into his forehead. Suddenly, he closed the phone and returned to their table, his expression grim. "I'm afraid I have bad news." He stared at the table as he spoke.

"What?"

"Our number one witness has gone missing."

"Maureen?"

The officer nodded.

"What do you mean by *missing*?" A stupid question, Alex realized, but he wanted to hear the officer's answer anyway.

"We can't locate her," he said, and then added, more quietly, "and she didn't leave a forwarding address."

"Do you think something's happened to her?" Alex avoided Tanner's eyes.

"Possibly, but I hope not. It could be that she's just chickened out and has gone into hiding." Alex had the distinct feeling that the officer was being more optimistic than he actually felt.

"Why haven't we been asked to be witnesses?"

"I'm not sure, Alex. Maybe because you are minors and have been through a lot already. But I suspect you will be now. Subpoenaed, no doubt."

"Subpoenaed?"

The officer nodded. "Required to testify. Not asked."

Alex stared at the officer as the truth of the situation sunk in. He pushed back his chair. "This sucks," he declared. "Maureen's gone, so now he's coming after us." He kicked the leg of the table. "I thought that crap was all behind us."

"Have you brought the letters with you, Alex?"

"Yeah." He pulled them out of his back pocket and slapped them on the table.

"The first one was made to look like it came through the mail," said Tanner, picking up the envelope, "but it hadn't been postmarked." He passed it to the police officer and then picked up the second envelope which contained the two sheets of paper. "We found this one in the mailbox this morning."

The officer pulled the letters out of their envelopes and studied them for a moment. Then he looked directly at Alex. "You've told your mom about this, right?"

"Wrong." Alex stared at the table.

"Why not?"

He looked up and met the officer's gaze. "She's already dealing with a divorce, a new job and a new city," he said. "I don't want to dump any more on her. I've screwed up her life enough already."

Officer Russell rested his hand on Alex's arm, but Alex tugged it away. "She needs to know what's going on, Alex," he said, ignoring the rebuff. "Are you still living with your uncle?"

"Yeah."

"He has to know too. It's his home these letters are coming to."

Alex nodded. He didn't have a problem telling his uncle about it.

Officer Russell tucked the letters back into their envelopes. "I'll give these to the investigators on this case," he said, stuffing them into his shirt pocket along with his phone. "They'll advise you on what to do. Hap is reporting to a bail supervisor and if he misbehaves he will be back behind bars. These letters," he patted his pocket, "may be all it takes to get him there — where he belongs, I might add."

"What if I just pay him back for the clothes?" asked Alex, beginning to feel desperate. "Do you think he'll leave me alone then?"

"Don't you dare, Alex. That's called extortion, so don't go there. Besides," he added bitterly, "if his gang could raise the bail bond just like that," he snapped his fingers, "it's not the money he's after."

Alex slumped down in his chair and folded his arms across his chest. This sucked, big time. He thought of running away again, but then remembered what had happened the last time he'd tried that. That was how he'd met Hap and gotten into this mess in the first place.

Officer Russell turned to Tanner. "You live in Edmonton, don't you? What brings you back to Vancouver?"

"I'm here for a hockey camp that starts tomorrow. And then I'm just going to hang out with Alex for a week."

"Hmm." The officer looked thoughtful. "It might be a good thing that you're both here together in case you need some protection ..."

"Protection?"

"Perhaps. I'm not sure what we can do ..."

Tanner glanced at Alex, who was staring at the floor, and then turned back to the officer. "I hope it doesn't affect our plans."

"Plans?"

"Yeah, we're going to search for our birth parents."

"Really? How come?"

"Well ... it's hard to explain. I just need to meet them. It would give me an identity. It's like there's this void ..."

"A void?" the officer queried, then turned to Alex. "What about you? Do you feel a void in your life too?"

Alex just shrugged. He picked at a hangnail.

"I guess it's natural to be curious about your roots," mused the officer, turning back to Tanner, "but it seems to me that we're all searching, trying to figure out who we are and where we fit into this crazy world. It's a lifelong pursuit. It's not the exclusive territory of adopted teens, you know."

"Yeah, I know, but Alex and I are different than other people because we used to think we were our parents' real kids."

"Real?"

"Yeah, real, as in biological."

"Biological kids are no more real to their parents than adopted kids."

"You know what I mean," Tanner said. "Anyway, we can compare how we felt before we knew we were adopted with how we feel now. And believe me, I feel way stronger about trying to figure out who I am now than I did before. There's this big question mark about my birth family."

The officer nodded thoughtfully and then glanced at Alex, who was looking more morose than ever. "Well," he said, "as long as you don't put yourself in any unnecessary danger ..." He glanced at his watch and stood up. "I'm due on the golf course in thirty minutes." He patted his breast pocket again. "I'll get back to you when I've turned these over to the investigators. We'll let you know if you're candidates for the witness protection program. In the meantime, you two are to watch yourselves, and if you see anything that looks at all suspicious, contact me at once." He reached into his back pocket for his wallet and pulled a business card out of it. He handed it to Alex. "Call my cell number, any time, day or night. Use your heads, your common sense and your intuition. And tell your mom, Alex. She needs to know. You too, Tanner. Tell your parents. I'll make sure the detectives keep you posted on any new developments. Any questions?"

Tanner shook his head, but Alex was studying the parking lot. Why were those people just sitting there in that black sedan? Officer Russell followed his gaze. Then he pulled a pen out of his shirt pocket and jotted the license plate number on a paper napkin.

seven

Tanner wove in and out of the pylons that were scattered across the ice, the blades of his skates making dull, scraping sounds on the chewed-up ice surface. He rounded the net, out-maneuvered one more pylon that stood guard in front of the goalie and roofed the puck into the upper left-hand corner.

"Nice move," commented the visiting pro, smacking the seat of Tanner's hockey pants with his stick as he skated by. Then he blew his whistle and announced the lunch break. Tanner glanced up into the stands where Mr. Bradshaw had reappeared a few moments before, carrying a bag of takeout food. He'd sat watching from the bleachers all morning and had only left long enough to pick them up some lunch. "I'll meet you outside after I strip down a bit," Tanner called.

A few minutes later he pushed open the arena door and squinted into the brilliant sunshine. He was barefoot and wearing only shorts and a T-shirt, but sweat was still running freely down the sides of his face. He joined Alex's uncle at a picnic table in the shade.

"You've got quite a talent there, Tanner."

"Thanks." Tanner washed down a mouthful of his hamburger with Coke. "But I don't think it's talent. Just hard work."

"I don't know. You're obviously a hard worker, but some kids just seem to have more natural ability than others do. Look at players like Gretzky and Lemieux. They worked hard too, but they also had something that set them apart from everyone else. It's something you're born with, I think."

Born with. Could you inherit a talent for hockey? And if so, Tanner wondered, had he inherited it from one of his parents? "That's why I'm going to search for my biological parents," he declared suddenly. "I want to know what I inherited from them."

Mr. Bradshaw stopped chewing for a moment and stared at Tanner. Eventually he swallowed his mouthful of food and took a long sip from his water bottle. "I don't think that's such a good idea."

"Why not?"

"You might not like what you discover."

"I'll take that chance."

"Is Alex in on this?"

Tanner nodded, but didn't make eye contact with Mr. Bradshaw.

"I'm surprised."

Tanner could feel the eyes studying him.

"He's not so keen, though, is he?"

The man was too smart. "No, but he'll come around."

They ate quietly for a few minutes. Tanner could see that Mr. Bradshaw was deep in thought. "How do you plan to go about it?" he asked, finally.

"I'm not quite sure, but I'll go to the library. There must be books on it. People do these searches all the time." He licked mayonnaise off his fingers. "I suppose I could even start with the phone book. There must be an adoption association I can contact." He scrunched the wrappers from his lunch into a tight wad and tossed them into the paper bag that stood open on the ground beside the table. "Did you see that? I have a talent for basketball too. Must be inherited."

Mr. Bradshaw ignored the awkward attempt at humor. "Have you told your parents?"

"Not yet, but I'm going to."

"And how do you think they'll take it?"

"They'll be okay. This doesn't have anything to do with how I feel about them."

"Maybe not, but they'll feel something, and it won't be a good feeling."

"What do you mean?"

"Everyone has their insecurities, Tanner. Your parents may put on a brave front and act supportive, but they're bound to feel threatened by the outcome."

"The outcome?" Tanner scratched his sweat-soaked hair.

"Yes. Your parents will wonder if they're going to have to share you after all these years, or worse, if you'll get hurt."

"They'll always be my mom and dad."

"You know that, and they know it deep down, but they're only human. They'll worry."

Tanner nodded. He'd never really considered their feelings. He'd have to reassure his parents that his search wouldn't change anything between him and them.

"My sister, Alex's mom. She's not going to like this."

"Yeah, that's what Alex said. That's why he's not going to tell her — not yet, anyway."

"Oh no. You have to tell her — now — before you start." Mr. Bradshaw banged his fist on the table. His face had turned crimson. "There's already been enough deceit concerning your adoption."

Tanner couldn't remember ever seeing Alex's uncle get so

worked up before.

"Besides," he said, trying to calm himself down, "she's got some very valuable information. Don't forget — she was there during the adoption."

Tanner smiled, trying to make light of the situation. "Good point. I'll talk to Alex about it tonight." He'd talk to him, all right, but it would be another thing to change his mind.

....

On the way home from the rink later that afternoon, Mr. Bradshaw invited Tanner to join him at the driving range. "We have time to hit a bucket of balls before I have to pick up Alex and Pat," he said.

Tanner politely declined, insisting he was too tired from playing hockey all day. He asked Mr. Bradshaw to drop him off at the house. He had a couple of hours before Alex and his mom would get home and if Mr. Bradshaw was out, he'd have the house to himself. "You go ahead," he suggested. "After my shower I might take a power nap."

As soon as he'd climbed out of the shower, though, he wrapped a towel firmly around his waist and pulled the phone book out of the desk where Alex had returned it just the day before. He looked up "Adoption". Sure enough, he found just the organization he needed — Adoption Reunion Registry.

He picked up the phone, then hesitated. He remembered Mr. Bradshaw's words. *You have to tell her — before you start.* He placed the phone back into its cradle but sat there, staring at it. What if they told her and she went ballistic? Would he have to give up his plan?

He couldn't take that chance. He wiped the palms of his hands on the towel and then punched in the numbers carefully. His stomach suddenly felt queasy.

The phone rang four times before it was answered.

"Hello. Adoption Reunion Registry. How can I help you?"

"Hi, yes. I would like to begin a search for my biological mother." There. He'd said it. This was easy.

"Could you hold, please? I'll put you through to the correct desk."

Music came over the line while Tanner waited. He'd waited so long that he'd begun to think they had forgotten about him when suddenly the music stopped and a voice caught him off guard.

"Hello, Corrine speaking."

"Oh, hi. I'm trying to find my mother." Oh man, he groaned to himself. Now he sounded like a little kid lost in a department store.

"I take it you're an adoptee?"

"Yes."

"And you'd like to be put on the registry."

"I guess. I don't know anything about this."

"What's your name?"

"Tanner Bolton."

"How old are you, Tanner?"

"Fifteen."

Tanner could hear the sigh in the pause that followed.

"That's what I was afraid of. You have to be nineteen to be put on the registry."

"You do?"

"Yes. That's the law."

"It is? Why?"

"Well, I guess the people who made these laws feel that teenagers are not mature enough to handle all the stuff that goes into doing a search. Successful reunions can be pretty traumatic, too."

"Well, I can handle it," Tanner replied, suddenly feeling angry at the assumption that all teenagers were the same, "and

I *have* to find her. What can I do?"

Corrine hesitated before answering. "There are ways, Tanner. It's hard work, but you can do your own search. I know of many successful reunions that resulted from private ones."

"How do I go about it?"

"The best thing to do is to get help from your adoptive parents. Do they support you in this search?"

"Yeah, I think they will."

"Good, because they can lead you to the social workers and lawyers who were involved in the adoption. They may also have some non-identifying information about your birth parents that will give you clues. You need to act like a detective. No information is insignificant. You have to snoop and question everyone you can think of. Do you know anything about the circumstances of your adoption?"

"Well, I'm a twin. My brother and I were separated at birth, but we've recently found each other."

"Really? It's unusual to separate twins. That information could prove to be very useful in your search."

"Yeah?"

"I'm an adoptee too, Tanner, so I understand why you need to do this. But remember, you've got to be prepared to live with whatever you find. If you aren't ready to accept that, don't bother to start it."

"Did you find your birth parents?"

"Yes, my mother. I had a lucky break."

"What was it like?"

"It was difficult at first. She'd tried to forget the period in her life when she'd had me. I made the initial contact and I think it was a painful moment for her. I guess she was curious about me, though, so we met, eventually, and established a kind of relationship. It's not perfect, but I no longer have that all-consuming desire to know about my roots."

"Yeah, like the one I have."

"Do you have access to the Internet, Tanner?"

"Yep."

"That's another good place to start. There are dozens of sites that allow you to register and promise to assist you in a search. But be careful. It isn't controlled and there are a lot of phonies out there. Don't invest too much money."

Tanner laughed. "I don't have much money. No need to worry about that."

"The library has good information, too."

"Yeah, I planned to go there."

Corrine sighed again. "Good luck, Tanner. You've just taken the first steps in a long, difficult and sometimes painful process. But I know where you're coming from. Some of us just have to do it. Give me a call if I can help you in some way."

Tanner thanked her, hung up the phone and sat back in the chair. He thought about everything Corrine had just told him. A slow smile began to spread across his face. It wasn't going to be easy, but he could do it. He'd begun and he knew exactly what he had to do. He'd phone his parents tonight and then call a meeting with Alex's uncle and mom.

He glanced at the wall clock. It would be another hour before Alex would get home. He studied the computer sitting idle in the corner of the room. Should he wait and get permission to use it? No, his time was limited. He went to the computer and pushed on the power switch.

.... eight

Alex bit into his sandwich as he watched the plane taxi down the runway, lift up and then disappear into a bank of clouds. If only he was on it, he thought. Destination: far away. He didn't care where, as long as he was away from this city and everyone in it.

He tipped a small carton of milk to his mouth and drained it. Was it only the day before yesterday that he'd sat here with Tanner, happily mapping out the next two weeks? Things had changed so fast. Tanner had arrived in town obsessed with the crazy scheme of searching for their birth mother. Listening to his brother's zealous sales pitch the other night he'd felt a twinge of curiosity, but now he could only see problems. One main problem, really: his mother.

His adoption was a taboo topic. Neither of them had mentioned it since the day last winter when he told her that he'd discovered he was adopted. She had apologized and explained why it was kept secret. Then the subject was dropped like a hot potato. No one had actually said it was taboo, but some things you just know. This was one of them. He also knew that having Tanner in their home made his mom uncomfortable — or was it sad? She'd become quiet and withdrawn since he'd arrived. Just wait until she found out what Tanner was planning to do now. No. Alex shook his head. He couldn't do that to her. He'd caused her enough grief in the past year. She must never find out.

That dilemma was bad enough and now Hap was back in his life, timed perfectly to spoil his holiday with Tanner. It had never occurred to him that Hap wasn't securely behind bars. The sense of safety he'd experienced over the past six months had vanished overnight. Hap had been out there the whole time. He wondered vaguely whether it was just coincidental that Hap chose to contact him the same week Tanner arrived in town or if it was planned that way.

Alex glanced around the cafeteria. He didn't see anyone watching him, but that didn't mean anything. The lady at the till could be working for Hap, or the man reading the newspaper at the next table ... He suddenly felt people staring at him from all over the cafeteria.

He jumped up. "You're losin' it," he told himself, but went back to work fifteen minutes early anyway.

....

"Where is he?" Alex demanded as soon as he hopped into his uncle's car that afternoon.

"Who? Your brother?"

"Yeah. Who else?"

"At home. Having a nap. He worked hard —"

"Alone?" Alex interrupted. "He's alone?"

John Bradshaw glanced sharply at his nephew. "Yes, he's alone. Who'd you think he'd be napping with?"

Alex's face burned as he shook his head. "Never mind. I just thought he'd be with you."

He knew they should have told his mom and uncle about Hap last night, but somehow he just hadn't been able to find the words. He'd kept imagining his mom's reaction when she heard the news ... the news that Hap was out there, sending them letters and watching them ...

She didn't deserve any more trouble, but, unlike Tanner's search, he knew, deep down, she did need to know about this.

Tanner met them at the door when they pulled into the driveway. He looked flushed, excited. Had something happened?

Alex grabbed a couple cans of pop from the fridge and gestured toward the patio. "Outside," he ordered.

They settled themselves in lawn chairs in a corner of the yard that was shaded by the branches of an ancient oak tree.

"Why did you stay home alone?" Alex snapped.

"What's the big deal?"

"Remember Hap? Maureen? Something could have happened to you!"

"Get a grip, Alex, the doors were locked. We can't go around being paranoid."

"No, but we have to be pretty damn careful."

Tanner nodded, somewhat sobered. "Okay. I did kinda forget for a bit."

"Don't forget again," Alex said. Then his voice softened. "How was hockey camp?"

"It was cool. Your uncle bought me lunch."

"Yeah, and?"

"And I told him about doing the search. I hope you don't mind."

Alex just shrugged. "And ... what else did you tell him?"

Tanner glanced at the house. He lowered his voice. "I didn't say anything about Hap. I know we agreed to do that together, tonight."

Alex nodded. "So what did he say about the search?"

"He said we had to tell your mom."

"Well, that's not going to happen."

"That's what I thought you'd say, so after hockey I got started. I went to the phone book, looked up adoption and there it was, a listing for the Adoption Reunion Registry."

Alex feigned interest in a bird splashing in a bird bath that hung from the branches of the tree. Once again he felt the tug of curiosity, but at the same time was afraid to hear anymore.

"Don't you want to know what happened?" Tanner asked.

"I'm not sure." Alex turned and looked directly at his brother.

"I don't get you," Tanner replied, shaking his head slightly. "This means so much to me. I can't understand why you don't feel the same."

Alex turned his attention back to the bird bath. More chickadees were there now, perched on the side, watching the first bird. "I just don't."

"Well, I'm going to tell you anyway. The woman at the Adoption Reunion Registry said we're too young to be put on the active registry, but suggested we conduct a private search and use the Internet as a starting place. So I did. I used your uncle's computer and it was incredible."

As Alex turned back to listen to Tanner he could see his brother's eyes begin to shine again. Tanner leaned forward in his chair as he continued. "There are dozens, maybe hundreds, of sites where you can register. I only had a chance to browse through a few, but there are tons of people out there doing searches." The words tumbled out faster and faster. "I can't wait to check it out again. I also read a couple of reunion stories from people who'd actually connected through the Internet. It was so cool."

The screen door to the patio slid open and Mr. Bradshaw

came through, fired up the gas barbecue and then closed the lid. Then he came over and sat down with the boys. "Got to burn off the grills for a bit," he explained.

Tanner glanced at Alex and then turned to face his brother's uncle. "There's something I want to tell you," he said. "I used your computer this afternoon and I surfed the Net a bit."

"You did? What were you looking for?"

"Just stuff on hockey. Anyway, I know I should have asked your permission. I'm hoping, if it's okay with you, I can use it and we can arrange some way for me to repay you."

"Go ahead, Tanner." He glanced at the house. "But remember what I said at lunch. You've got to talk to my sister about … that other thing, and the sooner the better."

Alex's heart sank. *That other thing*. Even his uncle couldn't bring himself to say the offending words. He pushed back his chair and stood up. "I'm taking a shower." He slammed the screen door shut as he went into the house.

He stood in the shower long after he'd finished washing, letting the pulsating stream beat the tension out of his shoulders. He closed his eyes and tried to clear his head. When he felt the warm water start to turn cool, he opened his eyes and shut off the taps. He hoped nobody else needed hot water for awhile.

Tanner was waiting for him in the room they shared. "You okay?" he asked.

"I guess," Alex replied. He rifled through a drawer. "Things are just going too fast for me. And I'm not looking forward to telling my mom about Hap."

Tanner nodded thoughtfully while watching Alex pull on his cut-offs and towel-dry his hair. "And as you heard, your uncle's insisting we also tell her about the search."

"Yeah, well, one thing at a time. Tonight we'll tell her about Hap." Alex didn't mention that he'd decided they weren't ever going to tell her about the search.

Tanner nodded. "I won't say anything to her but when I phone my parents tonight I'm going to tell them about it because Corrine said they might have some information they can share with me."

"Corrine?"

"She's the lady from the Adoption Reunion Registry."

"Oh."

"I'll tell them that not *everyone* knows about this search, though, okay?"

"Thanks."

There was a knock at the door.

"C'mon in," called Alex.

The door opened and Pat Swanson stood there, looking puzzled. "Phone for you, Alex. It's Officer Russell."

Alex forced himself to act like he got calls from police officers every day. "Thanks, Mom. I'll get it in the den."

When he hung up the phone a few minutes later he found the rest of his family on the deck; Tanner and his mom were setting the patio table while his uncle flipped salmon steaks on the barbecue. They all stopped what they were doing and stared at Alex when he joined them. Ignoring them, he glanced at the sizzling fish. "Is dinner almost ready?"

Mr. Bradshaw stared at Alex for a few more seconds. "Yes," he said, turning his attention back to the cooking fish. "Yes it is. C'mon, everyone. Bring your plates over."

Alex's mom brought out a potato salad, a green salad and a loaf of bread. She kept glancing at her son, but Alex wouldn't make eye contact with her.

Mr. Bradshaw tried, without success, to initiate some discussion during dinner. He described the hockey drills Tanner had participated in that day and recapped some of Tanner's better plays. Tanner smiled modestly but didn't add anything to the descriptions, and Alex and his mom nodded politely as they picked at their meals. Mr. Bradshaw eventually gave up and they ate in silence for a few minutes until Alex pushed his half-eaten meal away and broke the news.

"Hap's not in jail," he said. "His trial's not until September and he's out on bail."

John Bradshaw sat back in his chair. "How do you know this, son?" he asked.

"Because I got two notes from him. And Officer Russell confirmed it."

Alex's mom's fork dropped to the floor with a clatter. There was a long pause and Alex felt everyone's eyes on him — again.

"Is that why he was calling you tonight?" Mr. Bradshaw asked.

"Partly. We met with him yesterday and told him about the letters. He phoned to tell me that he turned them over to the investigators and that Hap's bail supervisor was notified. Hap denies sending them, of course. He also denies knowing what happened to Maureen. But if anything else happens his bail will be revoked."

"Maureen?" Mr. Bradshaw asked.

"Yeah. She's the witness who fingered Hap in the first place. She's missing."

Alex's mom shook her head slightly, as if coming to her senses. "What does Hap want with you?"

"We're not sure, but Tanner and I are going to have to testify." He looked at his brother. "And we *are* being subpoenaed." He turned back to his mother. "With Maureen gone, we're the key witnesses in this case."

Alex watched his mother's face as the significance of this sunk in.

"Are we going to be given witness protection?" Tanner asked.

Alex shook his head. "Get this. Because it hasn't been determined that anything has actually happened to Maureen, we don't qualify. It was decided that, given her history, it's more likely that she's just run off."

"Her history?"

"She was a runaway, too. That's how she hooked up with Hap. Officer Russell's not impressed, but he said there wasn't anything else he could do."

"So he knows where we live." Alex's mom's eyes darted about the yard, as if expecting to see Hap hiding in one of the shrubs.

"Pat, why don't we go relax in those lawn chairs?" John Bradshaw stood up and helped her out of her chair. "Alex, you put on the kettle and make your mom some tea. And perhaps you boys could clean up the kitchen again while we sit for a bit."

Alex and Tanner quickly piled the dishes on a tray while Mr. Bradshaw led his sister to a lawn chair.

In the kitchen, Alex grabbed the kettle and filled it with water.

"You were right about your mom," Tanner commented as he stacked the plates in the dishwasher.

"She's *my mom*. I *know* her." Alex glanced to see if his brother got his point, but Tanner didn't show any sign that he had.

"Did Officer Russell say anything about that black car, the one he got the license plate number for?"

"Yeah," Alex answered. "They were stolen plates. They've probably been tossed in a Dumpster by now." He poured the boiling water in a teapot, placed it on a tray with two teacups and pushed open the screen door with his shoulder.

Tanner had the dishes almost done by the time Alex returned from delivering tea to the adults. "I'm going to go into the den and phone my parents while your mom is outside," he said when Alex came back to the kitchen.

Alex nodded, picked up a tea towel and began to dry the few large bowls Tanner had set to drip-dry in the sink. As his brother left the room, he called out, "Good luck!" He could see Tanner's expression relax as he smiled.

"Thanks. I might need it."

Alex was waiting in the living room when Tanner came out of the den fifteen minutes later. "How did it go?"

"Good — for the first five minutes."

"What news did you break first?"

"I told them about the search."

"How did they take it?"

"Not bad. They said they were kind of expecting it. I guess they know me too well. In fact, they'd already dug the adoption papers out of the safety deposit box just in case I asked to see them."

Alex raised his eyebrows.

"They didn't tell me what's in them, but they said they'd stick photocopies of them in the mail tomorrow."

"You lucked out, I'd say."

"Yeah. I told them that you weren't sharing this with your mom for the time being."

"Thanks."

"I think I understand why, now."

"I thought it might become clear."

Tanner stretched. "Then I told them about Hap."

"And?"

Tanner chuckled. "I'm glad I couldn't see my mom's face. She didn't say anything at first, which is worse than having her rag on me."

"Yeah, I know what you mean." Alex got up and looked out the window to check on his own mom.

"What about your dad?"

"He suggested, very calmly, that I come home."

"What did you say?"

"I laughed and told him he was overreacting, that everything was under control."

Alex smiled. "Did he believe you?"

Tanner thought about it. "I doubt it. But he pretended to for my mom's sake."

"That was nice of him. Kinda like what my Uncle John did with my mom."

"So what are we going to do?"

"Do?"

"Yeah. About Hap. Do we have to stay locked up in the house for the rest of the summer?"

"Officer Russell said we'd be okay if we just use our common sense. Stay in public places, don't go off alone anywhere … stuff like that."

"Stanley Park's a public place. Look what happened there."

"Yeah, well, I don't know."

"Are you scared?"

"Yeah, a little. Actually, you were right. I *am* paranoid. Part of me, the scared part, wants to run away again, but part of me says screw him. He's not going to ruin our summer."

"I know what you mean. I wonder why he sent you those letters. Did he want you to run away or did he just want to scare you?"

"Probably wants to scare us. Keep us from testifying. But we don't have a choice — not now that we're going to be subpoenaed."

"I hope Maureen shows up."

"Me too. And not just her body."

"Do you really think … ?"

Alex nodded. "Look what he did to you. He was going to have you killed, then Maureen pulled a fast one on him. And you would have died anyway if we hadn't found you."

Tanner nodded. They sat quietly for a few minutes. Finally, he got up and stretched again. "You know, I don't really want to think about this anymore." He paused, thinking. "Did I see two bikes in the garage?"

"Yeah. You want to go for a ride? Didn't you get enough exercise at hockey today?"

"Actually, I'm sore everywhere. But we could go to the library. That would be safe enough. And then we could get started on the search. Is there a branch close to here?"

"Yeah, there is. I'll check with Uncle John about the bikes."

As the boys approached the adults, Alex was relieved to see that some color had returned to his mother's face. The tea and the warm summer evening had helped to numb the shock of Alex's announcement and she was smiling at something her brother had said.

"Who do the bikes in the garage belong to, Uncle John?" Alex asked.

"They're all yours if you want them. But tell me, Alex. What did the police say? Is it safe for you and Tanner to be out and about?"

"As long as we're careful, and we stick together."

"Where are you going?" asked Alex's mother. There were deep worry lines etched into her forehead.

"We thought we'd just go for a ride, maybe get some ice cream or something. We might go as far as the dike."

"Good plan." Mr. Bradshaw looked at his sister. "The dike will be crowded with people out enjoying the evening. They'll be safe there."

"We won't be late. Gotta work tomorrow."

They started back toward the house, but Mr. Bradshaw called after them. "Did you call home this evening, Tanner?"

"Yep."

"Everything go okay?"

"Just fine."

"See you later then."

Alex led the way down the street. The neighborhood was alive with people out gardening, walking dogs and chatting with one another. A couple of boys their own age zipped by them on in-line skates. They could hear the shrieks of children enjoying a game of kick the can. They rode slowly, side by side, savoring the warm evening. There was just enough of a breeze to keep it from being hot, and the knot of worry in Alex's stomach began to loosen, just a little.

But were they being followed? The knot tightened again. Alex glanced over his shoulder, but no one was paying any attention to them, or so it seemed.

Alex focused on his pedaling. He felt safe on the bike, in control; he could get away quickly if he needed to. If only they could spend the whole evening just cruising around, but he knew that when Tanner was on a mission there was no stopping him.

They arrived at the library a few minutes later and locked their bikes up outside before entering the cool, quiet building. Tanner went straight to a computer, typed in the word "adoption" and then pressed the search key.

Alex stood back, leaning against a bookshelf, checking for anything suspicious. His gaze rested on a girl working at a nearby table. She reminded him of Cara, his girlfriend when he lived in Tahsis on Vancouver Island. She had the same long, light-brown hair and fine features. She must have sensed she was being studied because she suddenly looked up and stared directly back at him. He felt a jolt of shock; her eyes were the same gray-blue color as Cara's, too. He blushed and glanced back at Tanner, but Tanner was also studying him, a smirk on his face. He approached Alex then, carrying a scrap of paper with a bunch of numbers written on it.

"We're here to do research, not to check out the chicks," he whispered. "C'mon."

Alex followed Tanner as he led the way toward the shelves of books. As they passed the table with the Cara look-alike he chanced another glance at her. Their eyes met and then she looked at Tanner. When she turned back to him, fascinated, he smiled tentatively. She smiled back, a shy smile, but a smile nonetheless. His heart raced. This time the fears and anxieties of the day *did* melt away, and he vowed he'd find a way to talk to her before they left that evening. Hurrying after Tanner, he completely forget to be on guard for anything suspicious, so he failed to notice the young man who left one computer and moved to the terminal Tanner had just vacated.

.... nine

Tanner studied the numbers on the spines of the books. He followed them along until he came to the ones he was looking for.

"Look at this, Alex," he called to his brother, who was dawdling at the other end of the aisle. "There must be twenty books on adoption. Everything from *Adoption Law and Legislation* to *International Adoptions*." He began pulling books off the shelf and leafing through them. "I don't know where to start."

"Well, you don't need books on *How to Conduct an Adoption* or *Raising Your Adopted Child*," Alex commented, coming up beside Tanner and glancing at some of the titles. "Why don't you choose a few that might be good and we'll take them over to that table and look through them."

"Yeah, okay," Tanner agreed before it dawned on him that Alex was suddenly acting too keen. "Oh I see." He dragged the words out. "I know what you're up to, you slimeball. You just want to get close to that girl."

"There's no harm in checking her out," Alex said, but Tanner could see him blush despite the attempt to act blasé.

"Okay, Alex, but don't be surprised if it's me she's hot for. I'm the better-looking one, remember?" he said, smiling. They began to pull books off the shelf and then walked, as nonchalantly as possible, back to the table where the girl sat absorbed in her work. Tanner glanced at Alex, eyebrows raised. Alex nodded, so they pulled out chairs across the table from her.

Tanner opened the first book in the stack and turned to the table of contents. He scanned the chapter titles until he came to "Chapter 10, Conducting a Search." He quickly opened the book to the correct page and began to read.

"Got any paper on you, Alex? There's a great list of stuff here. I've got to write some of it down."

"Well, I've got this old Kleenex you could use," Alex said, pretending to dig deep into the pocket of his shorts.

Tanner watched as Alex glanced across the table for the girl's reaction. She was smiling at Alex, but turned to Tanner. "I've got some paper you can use."

"Thanks." Tanner waited while she flipped to the back of her binder, tugged open the clasps, pulled out a few sheets of paper and passed them to him.

"Have you got a pen?"

Alex laughed, a little too loud. "That's my brother, always prepared."

The girl smiled as she passed him a pen she'd pulled out of her backpack.

Tanner ignored his brother and the girl as he jotted down the information: *Parent Finders, Adoption Resource Center, Canadian Adoption Reunion Register, Adoption Disclosure Register* and *Searchline*. When he was finished, he went back and added the addresses and phone numbers for each one. Then he put down the pen and began to rifle through some more books. He was aware of the small talk happening at the table, but was too engrossed in his task to pay any attention.

He picked up a book entitled *The Journey Back: Reunion Stories*. He began to flip through it and quickly became absorbed in a couple of the stories. He nudged his brother. "Listen to this, Alex. You know those papers my parents are sending me? It says here that one guy discovered the name of the town he was born in on the non-identifying papers. He knew the town was small, so it didn't take too much digging before he was able to find the names he needed."

He flipped a page. "And get this. This lady Jane says that she met with the lawyer that handled the adoption for her parents. She sensed he was hiding something so she kept pestering him until he disclosed the information. It turns out that years ago his secretary put her baby up for adoption. Jane was that baby. That's how she found her mother." Tanner looked up to see if Alex was as excited as he was but once again found Alex avoiding his eyes. The girl, though, seemed fascinated by what he was saying.

"You guys are adopted?" she asked Tanner.

"Yeah. But by two different families. We just found each other last winter."

"Really? Cool. How did you find each other?"

This time Alex did make eye contact with Tanner. He shook his head slightly.

"Well … you tell her, Alex."

Alex smiled. "So, now you know I'm Alex," he said, happy to change the subject. "And this is Tanner. You are …?"

"Caitlin." She stared at Alex, waiting for him to continue, but he picked up a book instead. "So, are you going to tell me how you guys found each other?"

Tanner watched Alex squirm, wondering why he didn't want to tell her. He decided to come to his brother's rescue. "It's a long, complicated story, Caitlin. We'd need a couple hours to explain it all to you."

"Oh." She flushed slightly, then glanced at her watch. "It's getting late. I've got to go."

Tanner watched Alex sit up, looking panicky. He decided to help him out again. "Perhaps we could tell you about it another time?"

She stuffed her books in her backpack. "Yeah, okay. How 'bout here — tomorrow night?"

"Perfect. Seven o'clock." Alex was all smiles again.

Caitlin smiled at Alex and then glanced at Tanner. "Keep the pen. I'll get it back tomorrow."

"Thanks," Tanner said. He watched Alex watch her walk away. He grinned and began to tap a rhythm on the table. "Just the two of us," he sang quietly. "We can make it if we try ..."

"Shut up."

"Shut up yourself." Tanner stopped singing, but he didn't stop grinning.

They read quietly for a few minutes. "A lot hinges on what those non-identifying papers contain," Tanner commented, serious once more. "I wish I'd told my parents to fax them to me."

"Hmm," said Alex, finally able to concentrate on what he was reading. "This guy simply put an ad in the paper and found his mom that way." He passed the book to Tanner.

Tanner read it, his excitement mounting. "We could do that."

"It costs money."

"Right, and you've got a job."

"Ha. I'm not spending my money on your project."

"Oh yeah. I do all the work while you go around picking up chicks. But when I make contact you'll be right in there."

"Maybe."

"Yeah, you will." He smacked Alex's arm before pulling out a fresh sheet of paper. "Let's write an ad. I'll figure out what to do with it later." He began to write.

Adopted twin boys, separated at birth, searching for birth mother. Born June 1, 1985, in Vancouver. Contact Tanner at 241-

7809 or at Bradshaw@aol.com.

"There." That reminded him of what he wanted to ask. "Why didn't you tell Caitlin how we found each other?"

"I don't know why — just a gut feeling I guess. It was weird; I suddenly had this creepy feeling, when I remembered that we can't trust anyone right now. You know how devious Hap is."

"You think she works for Hap? Get real! She was here before us tonight, and no one knew we were coming to the library."

"I know. But for a second there I just felt strange, that's all. I'll tell her our story tomorrow."

"Yeah, you are strange." Tanner grinned at his brother. "Whatever. I guess we can't check these books out or your mom might get suspicious." He looked around. "I'm going to shelve them in the wrong place," he whispered, "so I know they'll still be here tomorrow. Wait here."

Tanner wandered up and down the aisles of the library, pretending to browse. When he found himself in the sports section he looked around to make sure he was alone. Then he shoved the adoption books on the shelf. He'd remember this spot, no problem. His books were tucked snugly between the hockey and ice skating books. He took one last look around, assuring himself that he hadn't been seen, and then hustled back to join Alex at the work table.

But Alex wasn't there.

An adrenaline rush instantly jump-started his heart into erratic beating. Now *I'm* getting paranoid, he thought. But as he searched the library to no avail, the fear grew. Finally, he burst through the doors and glanced toward the bike rack.

There was Alex, straddling his bike with his arms folded across his chest. His head was thrown back and his eyes were closed as he soaked up the last few rays of the sun before it would sink behind Vancouver Island in the west.

"What the …?" Alex's eyes flew open and he struggled to regain his balance after receiving the shoulder check that was strong enough to have toppled him over, bike and all.

"What are you doing out here?"

"Waiting for you." Alex studied his brother's flushed face. "Oh, I see. You were worried. Thought something had happened to me, right?"

"You gave me hell for staying home alone today, and now I find you out here all by yourself? What's with you? What was I supposed to think?"

Alex smirked, though somewhat apologetically. "I thought you'd be right behind me. Where have you been?"

"Looking for you! Inside!"

"Okay, okay. I'm sorry. But at least now you know how it feels."

"Why'd you come outside?"

"I told you, I thought you'd be right behind me. Sorry." He paused. "Race you home," he suggested.

"Sure, loser," replied Tanner, snatching his bike from the

bike stand. "You don't stand a chance," he hollered over his shoulder as he pedaled across the parking lot. "I'm the jock, remember?"

Alex smiled to himself as he worked to keep up. You're right, he thought, but at least the distraction had worked. And he was glad that Tanner had been worried. Now he knew that Tanner would be on guard for anything suspicious.

....

Alex lay in bed, later, listening to Tanner's light snores coming from across the room. He wished he could simply doze off into an untroubled sleep like his brother. His own thoughts were so jumbled and confused that he didn't dare fall asleep and chance sending distress signals to his brother's dreams. He sat up and tried to figure out why the good mood he'd been in at the library had so quickly turned sour. He sighed. It didn't take long to figure it out. Meeting Caitlin tonight had been kind of fun, a thrill, but it had also reminded him of how much he missed Cara. It was like tearing open an old, unhealed wound, one that was festering away, just waiting to develop into a full-blown infection. Cara had been more than a girlfriend; she'd been his closest friend. He had Tanner now, but he still missed her. Why had he let her go so easily?

He quietly climbed out of bed and went down to the kitchen. If he couldn't sleep he might as well eat. He grabbed an orange from the fruit basket on the kitchen counter and plunged a knife into the thick skin to make a thumb hold. Dropping the knife in the sink he began to pace around the dark house while he peeled the orange. When he got to the den he flicked on a light and sat down in a chair. He dropped the peel on a side table and slowly pulled the orange apart. He popped one section at a time into his mouth, enjoying the explosion of sweet juice from each piece as he bit into it.

The phone was right beside him. He could pick it up and dial Cara's number ... No, it was too late. She'd be asleep. He finished eating the orange, licked his fingers and wiped his hands on his flannel shorts. Sitting back, he stretched out his long legs. The reflection of his movement in the computer screen caught his eye. He thought about Tanner's enthusiasm after surfing the Net that afternoon. That's it! he thought. He'd e-mail Cara a note. He still knew her on-line address from when they'd begun sending messages to each other two years ago, even though then they'd only lived a few blocks apart.

Alex flicked the switch on the computer and listened to the beeps of the machine as it dialed up the Internet. Should he be real casual and just ask her what was new? Tell her about his job and what he'd been doing? Or should he get right to the point and tell her how much he missed her? He decided to keep it light; he didn't know who might read her e-mail messages. If she gave him any indication at all that she still cared for him, he would write her a real letter, on paper, or phone her. A year ago, he realized, she knew him so well that he'd never be able to bluff his way around her with small talk. Would it take a long time to rebuild that kind of rapport? Would she even want to? And how would Tanner feel about him contacting her again?

The screen came up and Alex typed in her address. He took a deep breath and began the letter.

Hi Cara,

How's it going? Are you working this summer? My uncle got me a job at the airport. It's not bad — beats pumping gas. I guess you've heard that mom's living here now too. Dad's still hassling us but what else is new.

Got some lousy news yesterday. Turns out Hap — the guy who beat the crap out of Tanner — hasn't even been tried yet. He's out on bail. Pretty pathetic, isn't it?

Anyway, I saw someone who looked like you today and it made me wonder how you were doing. Send me a note, tell me what's new in Tahsis.

Alex

He reread the letter and frowned. It didn't say much, but he had to go slow. He wondered if he should put "Love, Alex," but decided against it. He pushed the Send command, waited a few seconds, then shut down the computer. He took the orange peels to the kitchen and dropped them in the compost bin that his uncle kept under the sink. Then he went back to his bedroom and climbed into bed. Writing Cara had been just the therapy he needed. He felt calmer now and knew he wouldn't be sending any distress signals to his brother that night. He hoped not, anyway.

....

The distress signals came the next day, and not in the usual way nor from the usual direction.

....

Alex was working in the tail section of a Boeing 727 toward the end of the afternoon when he was paged over the PA system. He hurried down to the cockpit where his crew supervisor waited, holding a cellphone out to him.

"Hello?" He'd never received a call at work before. It must be some kind of an emergency.

"Alex! Guess what?"

Alex recognized Tanner's voice but couldn't decide if it was excitement or anxiety that he heard in it. "What?"

"Your uncle didn't stay to watch my hockey today but two other guys were there, two guys I didn't know, and they were watching me."

"Now *you're* getting paranoid. They were probably hockey scouts, looking for some talent."

"No, they weren't! It was so obvious that they were watching me that one of the coaches asked me who my friends with the sunglasses were."

"They were wearing sunglasses? In the arena?" Alex noticed that Jim was staring openly at him now.

"Yeah!"

"Tanner, I've got to …"

"Something else happened too."

"What?"

"You got an e-mail message from Cara."

"Did you read it?"

There was a short pause. "Well, yeah. I saw who it was from so I didn't think you'd mind."

"Well, I do mind."

"Sorry. I won't do it again. But she said not to contact her anymore."

"She did? Why?"

"She said her parents saw your message and they told her she wasn't to have anything to do with you until the trial's over and Hap's behind bars."

Alex felt his face flush. "Since when did she start doing everything she was told?'

"Sounds like she's going to this time."

Alex heard Jim clear his throat and saw him look at his watch. "I've got to go Tanner. We can talk tonight." He hung up the phone.

"You're not supposed to take personal calls at work, Alex."
Jim's voice was gentle but firm.

"I'm sorry. It was sort of like a family emergency."

"A family emergency about sunglasses?"

"Yeah, kind of." Alex began to walk back to the rear of the
aircraft. "It won't happen again," he called over his shoulder. "I
promise."

....

When Alex got home he found his brother on the Internet. He
shut the den door behind him.

"Why'd you stay home alone again?

"Because of this." Tanner reached into his pocket and pulled
out two small vials with silver rings attached to one end.

"What are they?"

"Pepper spray. You can attach them to a key chain."

"Where'd you get them?"

"Your uncle bought them for us. Said we were only to use
them if we were getting seriously harassed or something."

Alex took one of the vials from Tanner and turned it over
in his hand.

"You have to twist the top," instructed Tanner, "and give it
a double click to activate it. That keeps it from going off unex-
pectedly." Alex nodded and then attached it to the key ring
that he kept in his pocket.

"Having it made me feel safe enough to stay home alone."

"It won't be much use against a gun."

"No, but it's small enough that no one will know we have it."

"Let's just hope we don't have to use it."

"I hear ya." Tanner turned back to the computer screen.

Alex dropped into a chair. "Where's the letter from Cara?"

Tanner passed him a sheet of paper. Alex skimmed it. Tanner had told him pretty much everything over the phone.

Everything, that was, except the stuff he could read between the lines. If it hadn't been for Hap he was sure she would have encouraged him to keep in touch. He crumpled the letter and threw the paper ball across the room.

Tanner swiveled around in the chair. "You okay?"

"No, I'm not. I'm totally pissed off. Hap's now controlling my love life. If he was in this room right now I'd …"

"You'd what, Alex?" Tanner didn't try to disguise his sarcasm.

"I'd kill him. I would!"

"Yeah right. One fifteen-year-old punk takes on the big-wig of organized crime in Vancouver."

"I would."

Tanner studied his brother thoughtfully. "What made you think of contacting Cara, anyway?"

"Oh. So you read my outgoing mail too?"

"Yeah. So?"

"So you're a jerk. Don't I have any privacy?"

"You've been an only child way too long. You've got a brother now. Get used to it. No more privacy."

"You'll be gone in less than two weeks."

"You didn't answer my question. Why'd you contact her again?"

"I just felt like it."

"After all this time?"

"It hasn't been that long."

"I thought you had the hots for Caitlin."

Alex sighed. "Maybe I do. But she also reminded me of how much I miss Cara. She was my best friend before I met you."

Tanner rolled his eyes, swiveled the chair back around and studied the computer screen again.

Alex stared at his brother's back. He thought about Cara's letter. She still cared about him, too, but now, because of Hap, she'd asked him not to contact her again.

He crossed his arms and thought about what Tanner had said. *One fifteen-year-old punk takes on the bigwig of organized crime in Vancouver.*

"Did you phone Officer Russell and tell him about those guys at the rink today?"

Tanner turned to look at his brother. "No, not yet. Why?"

"Well don't." His eyes narrowed. "I've taken enough of Hap's crap. It's time to play him at his own game."

"What?"

"You heard me."

"What are you going to do?"

"You mean what are *we* going to do."

"No, I mean what are *you* going to do."

Alex pointed to the computer screen. "You want help with your search?"

"Forget it, Alex. I already got beat up once for you. I'm not taking any more chances."

"What do you mean? You're takin' a chance just being here."

"Yeah, but they're not going to *do* anything to us."

"You don't really believe that, do you?"

"I'm trying to."

"Think about Maureen."

"She might have run away."

"If you believe that ..."

Tanner sighed. "So what are you going to do?"

"I don't know for sure yet, but I'm going to do something."

Tanner shook his head and faced the computer screen again. "Listen, Alex, you take on Hap, I'll search for our biological mother. I'll be there for you if you need me." He smiled. "Maybe. As long as I don't have to get the crap kicked out of me again. And you can help me when I need it. Deal?"

"Deal."

"Now, go get me those sheets of paper that you brought home from the library last night."

"What sheets?"

"The ones I got from Caitlin. You know," he said, "the ones that I wrote all that stuff on, and the newspaper ad."

"I haven't got them."

"Then where are they?"

"How would I know? Didn't *you* bring them home from the library?"

"No. I thought you had 'em."

"Why would I have them?"

"Because I left them on the table. When I got back, you were gone, and so were the papers. I assumed you'd taken them."

"Well, I didn't. I knew you'd be back."

"So who took them?"

Alex laughed. "Probably some other dummy who needed paper. Or some real efficient janitor."

"Damn. Now I have to start all over again."

Alex shook his head. He jabbed his finger in the air as he mimicked his father. "I hope you've learned your lesson, young man."

Tanner pulled the cap off his head and threw it at Alex. "Shut up."

Alex laughed, picked the cap up off the floor and slapped it on his own head. "Temper, temper."

Tanner shook his head. "I can see you're going to be a huge help with this search. Some deal," he grumbled.

.... eleven

Tanner found his stash of books right where he'd left them the night before. This time he decided to make photocopies of the pages he needed. When he finished he joined Alex, who was waiting by the door, watching for Caitlin.

"It's 7:15, Alex. I think you've been stood up."

"*We've* been stood up, you mean."

"Whatever. What do you want to do?"

Alex shrugged. "I don't know." He glanced at the pages Tanner was holding. "What are you going to do with those?"

"Use them for the search, what d'you think?"

"No, I mean, where do you plan to keep them? You can't let my mom get hold of them."

Tanner thought about it. Alex had a point. It wasn't like he was at home, where he could bury them in his desk or something.

"I know," he said. "I'll take out some books and keep this stuff stashed between the pages."

"You? Reading a book? That would look really suspicious!"

Tanner's eyes lit up. "Actually, I saw a couple books that looked good. I'll be right back." He returned to the section of the library where he had incorrectly shelved his books the night before. He reached down and pulled out two books: *Hockey Talk: The Jargon, the Lore, the Stuff You'll Never Learn From TV*, and *Slap Shots: Hockey's Greatest Insults*. He ran his finger along the row and then pulled out another book: *For the Love of Hockey: Hockey Stars' Personal Stories*. Perfect, he thought. These might even be worth reading.

At the checkout desk he realized he needed a library card.

"I'll be right back," he told the librarian, and left the books stacked on the counter. He found Alex sitting by himself on a bench outside.

"No sign of her?"

"No."

"Poor baby."

"Shut up."

Tanner laughed. "Do you have any ID?"

"Yeah, why?"

"I need you to do me a favor. I want to take out three books but I can't without a library card."

"So you want me to get a card and take them out for you?"

"Right. They're on the counter. I'll wait here."

"What's in it for me?"

"Nothing. Just do it."

"You owe me."

Alex was back a few minutes later, carrying the books. Tanner was pleased to see he was smiling — he'd been so serious the last few days.

"What's the joke?"

"That poor librarian," he grinned. "She thinks she's lost it. I didn't mention that I wasn't you."

"Yeah, so?"

"Well, she looked at me kind of funny, then said she thought I'd been wearing an Oilers T-shirt a moment ago."

Tanner laughed. "You didn't tell her?"

"No, I told her I didn't own an Oilers T-shirt. She just shook her head and gave me the form to fill out." He laughed again. "You should have seen her face."

"You're bad." Tanner grinned, took the books and pushed the folded pages he was holding into one of them. He was glad to see his brother wasn't too bummed out about Caitlin not showing up. He suspected that he was actually more disappointed than Alex was, but he'd get over it. He had enough to think about right now.

....

The letter Tanner had been waiting for arrived on Thursday. Alex's uncle had dropped him off at home after hockey camp and had left for the driving range. Tanner checked the mailbox on his way in. He flipped through the envelopes and felt his stomach lurch when he recognized his mom's familiar handwriting. He shoved the door open with his shoulder while ripping open the sealed flap. He pulled out two folded pages. The first one was a letter from his mom. He put it on the kitchen table to read later. He opened the second sheet. It was typed in an older-style font and on the top of it there was a return address for the Children's Aid Society of Vancouver. He scanned the single sheet briefly, then fell into a chair. It was too weird. Here was the information about the people that were his flesh and blood, his real family.

The top section contained information about his and Alex's birth. They were born at Grace Hospital with no complications. The birth weight was two thousand grams for Baby Number One and twenty-five hundred grams for Baby Number Two. He'd been told his birth weight in pounds and ounces so he didn't know whether he was the first born or the second. He hoped he'd been the first. He'd like to tell Alex that he was the older, more mature one.

Next there was a section about their mother. Tanner read it carefully. She was born in Canada in 1964 of English and German parents. She was 5' 7" tall with a slim build. She had blue-gray eyes and brown hair with reddish tints. Well, he and Alex certainly didn't get their eye color from her then. Their brown eyes must have come from their father's side, but the hair color was bang on.

He continued to read. She'd completed Grade 12 and was in nurse's training when she'd discovered she was pregnant and had abruptly dropped out of school. The babies' father was in medical school. The relationship had been brief and their mother had never told him about her pregnancy. She did not wish to involve him, feeling it might interfere with his career. She refused to name him.

Tanner put the page down and sat back. He could feel his heart pounding, as if he'd just come in from jogging. So his parents weren't idiots! They were both in the medical field, assuming his mother had gone back to nursing school. And his father didn't even know that he and Alex existed!

Tanner stood up and began pacing around the kitchen. Why hadn't his mother had an abortion? She certainly would have had the right connections. Maybe it was for religious reasons. Thank God she didn't, he thought. Had she planned to keep her babies and raise them herself?

Tanner sat back down in the kitchen chair and reread the information. He could see why it was called non-identifying. It went on to describe his mother's parents, their height and build, but there was no information about his father's side except that his mother believed his paternal grandparents were both in good health with no history of genetic disorders.

Tanner reached for the phone on the wall behind him. He had to phone Alex and share this news with him even though he'd promised not to phone him at work again.

There was a long wait before Alex came to the phone. Tanner could hear him being paged.

"Hello?"

"Alex. It's me."

"I told you not to call me at work." Alex's voice was low, not much more than a whisper.

"I know, but I just have to tell you about our birth parents. I got the papers from my mom today." Tanner waited for a response, but there was only silence on the other end of the line. "Alex?"

"Yeah, I'm here."

"It says that our mom was in nurse's training and our dad was a medical school student when Mom got pregnant."

"Your mom lives in Edmonton, Tanner."

"You know what I mean, Alex. But get this. Our *birth* mom never even told our biological dad that she was pregnant. He doesn't even know we exist."

"And?"

"Well, that explains a lot of stuff. If he had known about us things might have gone differently. We might not have been put up for adoption."

"No." Alex spoke so softly Tanner could hardly hear him. "We might have been aborted."

"Yeah, I thought about that too. That's another reason we have to contact her. To thank her. You know."

Tanner could hear Alex sigh on the other end.

"I've got to go, Tanner."

"Fine." Tanner slammed down the phone. He didn't get it. Why wasn't Alex as intrigued as he was?

Tanner noticed the other piece of paper that was lying on the table, still unread. He picked it up reluctantly. He really didn't want to know what his mom had to say about all this, but he began to read it anyway.

Dear Tanner,

Here's the information you wanted. I hope it satisfies your curiosity. I read it myself and couldn't help thinking about what an unselfish woman your birth mother was. That was quite a sacrifice she made to protect your biological father's career plans. She must have cared deeply about him. However, I also believe he had a right to know about the pregnancy but who's to know what factors were involved to complicate the circumstances.

Anyway, I'm sure glad she made the choice she did. I wish I could tell her how grateful your dad and I are for having had the opportunity to adopt you. I'm sure Alex's mom feels the same way.

I don't know how hard you plan to pursue this search for her, Tanner, but your dad and I will support you however we can. Please keep in mind, though, that corny as it sounds, giving you up for adoption was a gift of love, the greatest gift she could give you and us at the time, and sometimes it's best not to go back and rehash old business. Of course, my advice comes from the head and I know that your search must come from the heart. Your dad and I understand that you are not doing this because you are dissatisfied with us (I hope not anyway!) but that it is one of those things you just have to do. I respect that passion in you, Tanner. You've always been like that. Your intensity about things is one of the qualities I love most about you. No, that's not true. I love everything about you — even when you're driving me nuts!

Anyway, say hi to Alex, his mom and John for us, and keep safe!

Love, Mom

Tanner sat back and blinked, setting free a couple of tears from his brimming eyes. Trust my mom to get all gushy, he thought. He swiped at his eyes with his hands. Without meaning to she'd made him feel guilty about doing this search. In fact, she'd meant to do just the opposite, but it had backfired. And why did he need to do this when he had such a good family? Sure, his sisters made him crazy, but all sisters did that. It was not like his life was incomplete — it wasn't. He had everything he really wanted, especially now that he had a brother.

Tanner stared out the window that looked into the private garden of the backyard. A Steller's jay was hopping across the grass toward a pile of seeds that had fallen from the bird feeder. She was too cumbersome to eat directly from the feeder and had to hope for fallout from the chickadees' eating frenzies. He watched as another one landed on the fence and squawked a greeting to the first before joining in her hunt for uneaten sunflower seeds. Were they mates, perhaps foraging for food to feed their young? He thought about his dog again, and how she instinctively knew to feed her puppies.

Perhaps he should give up this idea of doing a search. That would make everyone happier. He could try again when he was nineteen. It would be easier then, and Alex might be more willing to help.

Some kind of message must have passed between the two jays because there was a sudden flutter of wings and they both flew up to perch on the fence at the same moment. Tanner hadn't heard a sound and nothing in the garden had stirred. Perhaps the birds could pass mental pictures to each other the way he and Alex could.

Was that something they had inherited from their mom or dad, he wondered, or was it simply a part of their being identical twins? He had so many questions and so few answers. No, he couldn't wait another four years. He had to continue with this search even though he now understood why his mother had to put them up for adoption. In fact, he almost felt more urgency to continue with it, if for no other reason than to thank her for not choosing abortion.

Tanner went to the den and turned on the computer. He waited while it dialed up the Internet and then punched in the words "Adoption Search." Moments later the screen changed and a long list of sites pertaining to adoption appeared.

Over the past few days he had systematically browsed through the list of sites and had registered his name for a search wherever he could. But the information seemed endless, with chatrooms, discussion forums and many, many reunion stories. He read them all. He found the spot where he had left off the day before and clicked the mouse on the next entry: Adoptee Search Center. Once again, Tanner began to read ...

.... twelve

Alex hung up the phone and went back to cleaning the interior windows of the plane. He tried not to think about his brother's news, but his mind kept replaying one thing Tanner had said: *He doesn't even know we exist.* How ironic, he thought, that his biological father didn't know he had created life — two lives, in fact — while his adoptive father had tried so desperately but unsuccessfully to have a son of his own. Alex was sure that his problems with his dad stemmed from the fact that he was adopted. He knew he was a disappointment to his father, otherwise why would he have treated him the way he did? No one would treat his or her own flesh and blood that way.

The window squeaked under the rubber squeegee Alex used. He wondered what his brother would do next. Tanner was lucky, he thought. There were so many options available to him to help with his project. Alex's own project was going nowhere. His ambitious plans to get even with Hap had not even begun to take shape. What could he retaliate with? The only power he carried was his ability to testify at Hap's trial. But then, hadn't Maureen carried the same power? And how powerful was she now?

What *had* happened to Maureen?

Alex felt a surge of guilt wash over him again. It was his fault if something had happened to her. She'd turned Hap in because of what he'd done to them, him and Tanner, and now she was paying the price — one way or another.

But had he killed her? Perhaps she was being held hostage, or maybe she really had run away. If she was alive and able to testify, then they'd have a much better chance of getting Hap convicted in September. Maureen's testimony would carry a lot more weight than his and Tanner's alone. He had to find out.

Hap's men, Alex thought as he scrubbed with a vengeance, had followed Tanner to the hockey rink. Where else had they been? Perhaps they were following them everywhere. If that was the case, Alex just had to be real observant, spot them and … make contact? A plan began to take shape. It was danger-ous, but he had to do something.

He decided to start that evening.

"Let's go to a movie," he suggested as he and Tanner loaded the dishwasher after supper.

"Forget it. We're going back to the library."

"We've done that twice this week. We need a break."

"No, we don't," Tanner argued. "We don't have much time. We need to get through all the adoption sites on the Internet. We can use the computer at the library."

"Listen, Tanner. I've agreed to help you with your search, but now you've got to help me with my plan."

"And what plan is that?"

"I'm just working it out. But I need to make contact with Hap, or one of Hap's people, and find out if Maureen is alive or not."

Tanner shut the dishwasher door and stared at his brother. "You're serious?"

"Uh-huh."

"I thought we were playing it safe."

"We are. We'll still be in a public place, we'll be together, and ..." he reached into his pocket and pulled out his pepper spray, "we've got this."

Tanner shook his head. "Okay," he agreed reluctantly. "Tonight's your night. But tomorrow we go back to the library."

"You're on."

....

Their walk to the theater was uneventful, but as Alex scanned the crowd queued outside the theater he noticed Caitlin and another girl crossing the street and approaching the end of the line. His body language must have shifted abruptly because Tanner quickly peered toward the crosswalk to see what Alex had seen.

"Hey, it's Caitlin," Tanner announced, sounding pleased.

"Yeah, Caitlin-who-stood-us-up-at-the- library," Alex said. "Let's get out of here before she sees us." He tugged at Tanner's T-shirt, trying to drag his brother away. But Tanner held his ground, his gaze still on the girls coming toward them.

"She's probably got a logical explanation," Tanner said. "And if not, let's watch her squirm."

Alex would have liked to avoid the scene altogether, but it was too late. The girls were almost upon them and would have noticed them walking away.

"Not bad," Tanner whispered, sizing up the other girl. "Hey Caitlin," he called as they approached.

Alex watched Caitlin's face as she heard her name and spotted them in the line. He saw her flush and avert her eyes. She looked embarrassed all right, but there was something more in her expression. Was that fear he saw?

The girl she was with saw them watching Caitlin and quickly nudged her over. Caitlin didn't have a choice but to face up to them. Alex found the nervous giggling of her friend annoying but felt sorry for Caitlin. He hated confrontations. He glanced at Tanner, though, and saw him enjoying the moment immensely.

"We missed you the other night, Caitlin," Tanner said. "I wanted to return your pen."

"These are the twins you told me about?" asked her friend. She giggled again and Alex quickly looked her over. She had a row of tiny gold hoops imbedded into one of her eyebrows, which arched above heavily shaded lids, the colors matching the streaks in her closely cropped, bleached-blonde hair. Not bad? *Too weird*, would be the way he'd describe her, although, admittedly, he found it hard not to stare. And she did radiate a certain irresistible energy.

"Sorry about that," Caitlin said, answering her friend with only a nod. "Something came up."

"We gathered that," Tanner said. "Too bad."

"Yeah," answered Caitlin.

They stood in awkward silence for a moment.

"How 'bout introducing us to your friend?" Tanner suggested finally.

She shrugged. "This is Zoe," she said unenthusiastically. She looked at Tanner. "You're Tanner, right?" she asked. Tanner nodded. "And this is Alex," she said, making eye contact with him for the first time. Their eyes locked for a moment too long and he wished he could understand the confusion he saw there.

"So are you guys going to the movie too?" asked Zoe. She directed the question to Tanner.

"Yeah. Unless you can suggest something better," he answered, encouraging her to do just that.

Zoe was up to the challenge. "Going to a movie was Cait's idea," she said. "I suggested we do something else, like something outdoors. It's such a nice night. But, like, she wanted to come here. Maybe we can get her to change her mind." She grinned at Tanner and they both looked at Caitlin.

Caitlin shrugged. "Whatever."

Tanner and Zoe turned to Alex. "Whatever," he said, not meaning to imitate Caitlin but realizing, too late, that he had. Her glance told him she thought he was making fun of her, so he quickly apologized. "I didn't mean it that way," he said, ignoring Tanner's laugh and Zoe's silly giggle. "It was my idea to go to the movie, too, but I'm easy."

"That's what he always says," laughed Tanner. "But don't believe him. He's actually a real prude."

Zoe burst into another fit of giggles and tugged at her snug miniskirt. Caitlin looked at Alex, rolled her eyes, and Alex knew that he was forgiven.

"What should we do then?" Alex asked, anxious to redirect the conversation.

"I thought we should get some slushies and spits and go over to the park. There might be a game tonight," said Zoe. "But, like, Caitlin's been acting weird all week. She doesn't want to go anywhere! She's, like, allergic to the sun or something."

"The park," Tanner said. "Good idea." He turned to Caitlin. "Can we change your mind?"

She thought about it. "I guess," she said, frowning. Tanner ignored her hesitation and started across the parking lot to the convenience store. Zoe quickly caught up to him, and Caitlin and Alex followed behind.

Zoe jabbered nonstop all the way to the park, and Alex noticed how relaxed and comfortable Tanner appeared to be with her. Caitlin, on the other hand, hadn't said a word and Alex didn't know how to break into her stony silence. He couldn't remember ever feeling so awkward and tried to remember what he might have said at the library the other night to make her so cold and distant.

There was a game being played at the park and it appeared

that the whole neighborhood was out to see it. Zoe recognized some of the players and grabbed Tanner's hand, pulling him up into a tiny opening in the packed bleachers.

Alex watched Tanner scramble up behind her, then turned to Caitlin. "It's a bit crowded up there." He looked around the field and noticed a huge willow tree off to one side, near the chain-link fence. "Want to go sit over there, under that tree?"

Caitlin nodded, looking relieved, and they walked away from the crowd, Alex silently cursing Tanner for leaving him alone with this girl who obviously didn't want to be with him in the first place. The tree trunk was wide enough for them both to lean against, but Alex wanted to give Caitlin enough space so that their arms wouldn't accidentally brush together, so he sat cross-legged beside the tree. The silence continued for a few minutes; they sipped their drinks and stared off toward the game that they really couldn't see very well from where they were. Tanner and Zoe had taken the bag of sunflower seeds with them.

"Do you like baseball?" he finally asked, just to break the silence.

"Not really."

"Me neither." They both laughed, and Alex sensed she'd relaxed, just a little.

"We're the suckers, then, aren't we?" he said.

"Yeah, I guess. Zoe has a way of getting me into these kind of situations."

"So, why do you hang out with her?"

Caitlin smiled. "Because she's fun. There's never a dull moment when you're with Zoe. The question is, why does she hang out with me? I'm so boring."

Alex glanced at her, wishing he could tell her how much more appealing he found her than Zoe, but knew it would be unwise. "You know what they say," he answered lamely, "opposites attract."

"Yeah."

They stared into the distance, silent again.

"So, are you still looking for your biological parents?" Caitlin asked finally.

"Yeah." Alex was surprised at the question. "Actually, Tanner is. I'm just helping him."

"I used to think I was adopted."

"You did? How come?"

"Because I don't look like my brother or my sister, or anyone else."

"But now you know for sure you aren't?"

She nodded.

"Were you relieved when you discovered you weren't?"

Caitlin didn't answer right away. She turned and looked directly at Alex. "Yes and no," she said thoughtfully. "I kind of enjoyed the idea of being different. I'm the middle child, the second daughter, and there's nothing special about that. I thought being adopted would make me unique."

"But you said you were kind of relieved to find out you weren't, too?"

"Yeah, thinking that I'd been lied to all those years bothered me."

"That's what bothered me too. And I have my father to thank for that."

"Sorry I didn't show up the other night." It came out of nowhere, and Alex glanced at her, noticing the scarlet cheeks.

"That's okay, no big deal."

"No, it's not okay. It was rude. But ..." She glanced at him, and he could see the troubled expression back in her eyes. "Something happened when I left the library and I was too nervous."

Alex felt like someone had just kicked him in his stomach.

"I should have come and told you, though," she continued. "I wanted to ... but I got scared."

"What happened?"

"Well, I was walking home when this car pulled up beside me and this guy got out and started asking me a bunch of questions about you and Tanner."

"Damn!"

"Why was he asking me all that stuff?"

"We've got some guys pissed off at us. What'd you do?"

"Nothing. He kept pestering me but I kept walking."

"What was he asking?"

"If you were going away, how long Tanner was staying and a bunch of other stuff. I guess I finally convinced him that I really did just meet you and eventually he gave up, went back to his car and drove away."

"Oh man, Caitlin. I'm really sorry." Alex got up and paced nearby.

"It's not a big deal, Alex." Caitlin watched his agitated movements. "I'm just such a chicken. I figured it would be best not to see you guys again. But I should have come and explained that all to you."

"No you shouldn't have. You didn't owe us anything." Alex crossed his arms over his chest. "I should have left you alone in the first place."

"What do you mean?"

He didn't answer but sighed and sat down beside her again.

"Who were those guys?"

Alex pulled a long blade of grass out of the ground, stuck one end in his mouth and chewed on it for a few moments. He didn't know how much to tell her.

Caitlin smiled and rested a hand on his arm. "Some dog probably peed on that grass, you know."

Alex laughed, despite himself, and chucked the grass away. "Remember you wanted to know how Tanner and I found each other?"

"Yeah. And you wouldn't tell me."

"That's right. Tanner said it was a long story, which it is. But that guy who was following you is part of the story."

"Really?"

"Yeah. In fact ..." Alex's eyes scanned the field and park. "I'm one hundred percent sure they're here somewhere, watching us right now."

Caitlin looked around, frowning. "Who's *they*?"

Alex didn't know where to start with the story. He looked over to the crowded bleachers where he could see Zoe practically sitting on Tanner's lap as they watched the ball game.

"You know, Caitlin, maybe you shouldn't be seen with me."

"Why not?"

Alex stood up, suddenly overcome with a sense of shame. "Damn." He kicked the trunk of the tree, hard. "I'm a real jerk to even be here with you. Why don't you go sit with Zoe and I'll drag Tanner home?" He offered her a hand to pull her off the ground, but she just sat there, nervously twisting the fine gold chain that she wore around her ankle. Finally he crossed his arms and stared off into the distance, waiting for her to decide whatever it was she was contemplating.

"I'd like to hear your story, Alex."

Alex looked down at her. Her head was still bent forward, and from this angle it was uncanny how much she looked liked Cara. He squatted down, forcing her to look up and face him. "I don't want to put you in any danger."

"I'll take that chance." She swallowed hard. "I'm tired of always being a chicken."

He offered her his hand again to pull her up. This time she accepted it, but just until she was standing. "You're sure?" he asked.

She nodded, looking directly into his eyes.

....

"Well, don't we look cozy."

Alex looked up, startled. He hadn't heard Tanner and Zoe approaching. He and Caitlin were sitting in swings at the playground, their arms linked at the elbows and their heads pressed together as they talked. He'd just finished telling her all about the events that had brought him and Tanner together last winter.

"You're going to like this story, Zo," Caitlin said.

"What story?" Zoe's eyes lit up.

"The story of how these two met. It's just your thing. Weird and wild. And it's not over."

"Cool. Start talkin', guys."

So Tanner told the story again as they walked back to the theater, where Caitlin's parents were picking up the girls.

"So now he's following you guys, and he followed Caitlin too?"

"Yeah. We figure he's trying to intimidate us."

"Cool."

"And now Alex wants to make contact with him."

"No way."

"Yes way. Right, Alex?"

Alex nodded.

"Awesome!" Zoe's eyes shone. "Can I help? I love this kind of stuff."

Alex glanced at her, bouncing along beside him. Caitlin is right, he thought. They are opposites. Complete opposites, right down to body types. "You're hired," he said, caught up in her enthusiasm. "I'm gonna need all the help I can get." But then he glanced at Caitlin and felt a pang of guilt. She was biting her lip and looking anything but enthusiastic. He hoped she wouldn't regret her change of heart and think that being a chicken hadn't been so bad after all.

thirteen

"I think she wants me, Alex."

Alex snorted and then had to fight to swallow the mouthful of Coke that had almost exploded out through his nose. "Yeah. That was pretty obvious last night."

"What am I going to do?"

Tanner sounded so pathetic that Alex had to cover his mouth with his pillow to keep from waking up his mom and uncle with his laughter. It was late Friday night. Tanner had been to a hockey-camp windup, a pizza and video party, and had only been home a few minutes. Alex had just reported that Zoe had phoned him three times throughout the evening.

"What do you *want* to do?"

"I don't know. She's pretty wicked." He thought back to how close to him she'd sat in the bleachers at the ball game. It was crowded, but not *that* crowded. What was he supposed to think? "What's happening with Caitlin?"

"I don't know. It's strange. Have you ever liked two people at the same time?"

"Nothing weird about that."

"It's weird for me."

"Yeah, but I keep telling you. You're a loser." Tanner chucked his pillow at his brother and changed the subject. "We're on holidays. It's party time! Let's do something to mark the occasion."

"Like what?"

Tanner thought about eating again, but he was still stuffed from all the junk food he'd devoured at the hockey party. "Let's do something ... bad."

Alex grinned. "Bad? Sounds like you still have Zoe on your mind."

Tanner laughed. "Maybe I do." He studied his brother. "Do you want to hit some hot sites on the Internet?" he whispered conspiratorially.

Alex's eyes lit up as he chucked the pillow back. "Perfect."

Tanner led the way down the hall to the den. Alex quietly closed the door behind them. When the Internet had been dialed up, Tanner decided to check for e-mail messages before surfing the Net. He clicked on the envelope icon and the screen immediately showed that there were two new messages waiting. The first one was already displayed. With Alex peering over his shoulder, Tanner read,

Subject: Twin Research

Dear Twin,

In our continuous quest to understand the role genetics plays on human development, we are again conducting a study of monozygotic twins at the Genetic Resource Center at the University of British Columbia this coming week and require 20 sets of identical twins. For your time you will be paid $100 each. Please call 822-7500 or reply by e-mail if you would like to participate in this important study.

Dr. Richard Montgomery

"What are monozygotic twins?" Alex asked.

"Beats me," Tanner answered. "But what I'd like to know is who at UBC knows there are twins at this address."

Alex just shook his head, puzzled.

"I wonder." Tanner stared at the message. "I've been leaving this e-mail address at a lot of adoption search sites. Could someone get it from one of them?"

Alex shrugged. "I don't know how these things work."

"Well, whatever," Tanner said. "You want to go for it?"

"Let's give 'em a call tomorrow and find out more about it. It might be kinda cool."

Tanner clicked on the icon to bring up the second piece of mail. It had no subject, but all thoughts of surfing the Net vanished when he read the first line.

Dear Son (?),

For the last year I have been using the WWW to try to locate my twin boys that I put up for adoption 15 years ago.

"Holy shit." Tanner glanced at Alex, but Alex couldn't take his eyes off the letter. Tanner continued to read.

I saw your posting this afternoon and am trying to stay calm. Might I finally see you again after all these years?

Here's my story. I gave birth to identical twin boys at Vancouver Grace Hospital on June 1, 1985. Because I was a single mom, I was talked into giving you up for adoption but not a day has gone by that you are not in my thoughts. I pray that I have found you at long last. However, we must proceed with caution. I have a new family now and they know nothing about this, but I must see you again — you have no idea of the pain I've suffered because of my decision to put you up for adoption.

If you believe you are one of my twin boys, please post a note in the Findme site and I will watch for it.

YBM (hopefully)

"Holy shit," Tanner said again and slumped back in his chair. "What is YBM?"

"Your Birth Mother."

"How do you know that?"

"I've been doing the research. I know the lingo." Tanner turned to face his brother, who had flopped into his uncle's reclining chair, his arms crossed, face flushed.

"So. You must be thrilled."

Tanner ignored the sarcasm. "I should be, shouldn't I?" But he wasn't. Tanner drew in a deep breath and tried to calm the fluttering in his stomach. Everything he'd read said that this kind of search would take months, probably years.

It had only been one week.

He wasn't ready for this. He turned back to the computer screen and reread the letter. "It must be her. How many other women would have given birth to twin boys on June 1, 1985? And even if someone else had, what are the chances that two sets would have been given up for adoption on the same day?"

"I didn't say I doubted it."

"I wonder why she can't tell her family about us?" Tanner mused. Something about that part of the letter didn't sit well with him. If she really had agonized over giving them up and had gone to the trouble to search for them, why wouldn't she have the courage to tell her family? What was she afraid of?

"So, what are you going to do now?"

"I don't know. I'm not ready for this. I need some time to think about it."

"You're keeping her waiting."

Tanner glanced at his brother. "Shut up."

"Shut up yourself."

Tanner printed off a copy of the message and shut down the computer. "What would you do if you were me?"

"I wouldn't have started this thing in the first place if I wasn't prepared to follow it through."

"You mean you want me to contact her? Set up some kind of reunion?"

"No, I mean do what you want. But you can count me out. I'm not going to meet her."

Tanner's mouth dropped open. "Alex! This is your mother!"

Alex leaned closer to his brother. His eyes were narrowed and he practically spit out the words. "My mother is asleep down the hall. That woman," he pointed at the blank screen, "chose to give us up. She didn't want us enough to keep us, remember? I don't know why you want to give her the satisfaction of meeting you now."

"I see. You want to punish her."

Alex didn't comment.

"But you read the letter. She's been miserable all these years. She needs to know us. We could at least correspond with her."

"She made her choice over fifteen years ago. Now she has to live with it."

"Why are you being such a jerk? She made a bad decision — once. And now she's trying to repair some of the damage. Like you've never made a bad choice?"

"Yeah, I have." Alex stared at his brother and swallowed hard. "And now I'm living with the consequences. And there's nothing anyone can do to take back what I did."

"What are you talking about?"

Alex stood up and stared down at his brother. "I chose to

meet Hap, I fell in his trap and now I'm still paying for it. I suspect I may be paying for it for the rest of my life."

"That's completely different." Tanner stood up to face his brother. "Our mother's only mistake was to get knocked up in the first place. And I'm sure that wasn't her choice. Giving us up for adoption was an ... an act of love."

"Oh yeah, I forgot." Alex switched to a sugary-sweet voice. "An act of love." He shook his head. "Call it what you want, Tanner. But now she has to deal with it."

"I think *you're* the one who has to deal with it." He shoved Alex's shoulder. Alex shoved back, hard. Tanner lost it. He threw his whole weight at his brother and they both went sprawling into the easy chair. There was a flurry of fists, and elbows flew as Tanner tried to climb off, but before he could the door to the den swung open. Alex's mother stood there, rubbing sleep from her eyes.

"What's going on here?" she asked, a hint of anger in her voice.

The boys glared at each other. Tanner shoved himself away from Alex.

"Nothing."

"Really?" John Bradshaw had come up behind his sister. His hair was tousled from sleep but he looked amused at finding them in the middle of a fight. "Well, if nothing's happening here, then let's all go back to bed." He studied the boys for another moment. "Alex, maybe you'd like to sleep on the sofa in here tonight. Give your brother a little space."

Alex nodded. Tanner watched him glance at the sheet of paper still on the printer.

"After you then, Tanner," said Mr. Bradshaw, standing back to let him pass through the door. "Good night, Alex. Sweet dreams."

Tanner didn't actually look at Alex's mom as he slunk through the doorway, but he felt a pang of guilt when he brushed by her. He wondered if she had heard any of their conversation and he could see she was hanging back, perhaps to talk to Alex. As steamed as he was at Alex right then, he still hoped Alex didn't have to 'fess up to what they'd been fighting about. That would just make Alex even more irate. And deciding what to do next was going to be hard enough without having Mrs. Swanson's messed-up feelings involved.

.... fourteen

"What's going on, Alex?" Pat Swanson remained in the doorway after Tanner and his uncle had gone back to bed. She
looked tired and very fragile in her pale blue nightgown, her
hair curling loosely around her face.

"Nothing, really. Just … a disagreement." Alex was acutely
aware that Tanner's letter from their birth mom still sat on the
printer. He had to reassure his mom that everything was okay
and get her out of the den. But instead she moved further into
the room and sat in the office chair. The printer was right beside her elbow.

"You're sure there's nothing you want to talk about?"

"No, really, I'm fine." He tried to smile, but his lip felt like
it might be swelling up from a jab it took from Tanner's elbow.

"Are things not working out between you and Tanner?"
She sounded almost hopeful.

"Things are fine, Mom. Don't worry."

"Things didn't look so fine when we came in here a few
minutes ago."

"Yeah, well, I'm not used to having a brother." He racked

his brain, trying to think of some way to quickly change the subject and keep his mom's eyes focused on him rather than wandering around the room, possibly to stop at the page sitting on the printer. "Tanner and I may take part in a study being done at UBC next week. The researchers need twenty sets of twins."

"Really? How did they find you two?"

"I'm not really sure. Through Tanner, I think."

"And that's how you want to spend your week of holiday time?"

"Yeah, maybe. We have to get some more information about it. But they pay $100.00." Money talked when it came to his mom. They didn't have much — not until the divorce was settled. "And it might be interesting."

"Hmm." Pat Swanson studied her son. She shuffled her bare feet a couple of times. Alex wondered what was on her mind. He didn't have to wonder long. "Have you been contacted by those criminals again?"

So that was it. "No." He couldn't believe he could look her straight in the eye and lie so easily, but it was for her own good, he told himself, trying to justify his answers, and they really hadn't *contacted* him.

"We could return to Tahsis, you know. Your father would still take us back."

"Mom!" He stared at her, his mouth gaping. "Have you lost it?" Had she?

"I'm just thinking of your safety."

Alex wondered how his mom would react if she found out Hap's reach easily extended as far as Tahsis. "Since when was it safe living with Dad?"

"I know how you feel." She leaned closer to Alex and took both his hands in her own. "But at least we know what we're dealing with there. And he claims he's changed. He doesn't threaten me anymore." It sounded like she was trying to convince herself. He felt a wave of sadness wash over him. His mom would happily move back in with his dad if she thought she could protect him. There probably wasn't anything his mom wouldn't do for him, but her options were so limited.

"After the divorce the court will probably allow him visitation rights, you know," she said, releasing his hands.

"I know. But *I* don't have to show up."

"I think you do."

"Nobody can make me."

"He loves you, Alex."

"He has a funny way of showing it."

"Yeah, he does."

They sat in silence for a few minutes. Then his mother spoke again. "I'll go get you a blanket, honey, and a pillow. We better get some sleep."

The moment she walked out of the room Alex jumped off the couch and grabbed the letter from the printer. He quickly shoved it into a desk drawer and then went down the hall to the bathroom. When he returned he found his mom had made a cozy bed for him and she was gone, probably back to her own room. He pulled the blanket up to his chin and tried to empty his mind of all the stuff that had gone on in this room that evening. Suddenly, an image of the trophy was in his head. He smiled to himself. Perhaps that was Tanner's way of apologizing. He focused on the picture, sending it back. Tanner would know that everything was okay.

....

Alex slept late the next morning. When he finally did get up he found Tanner chatting with his uncle on the sundeck. He pulled up a chair to join them, wondering if Tanner was disclosing the information he'd received via e-mail the night before. But they were talking hockey and Tanner nodded at Alex when he joined them. Alex sensed it was safe to assume the fight was over.

He heard the phone ring in the house and then Alex's mom called out the open window, "Tanner, it's for you."

Alex grinned. "Wonder who that could be?" Under his breath he added, "Lover boy."

Tanner pinched Alex's arm as he walked past him but Alex let it go.

"You two are finally starting to act like brothers."

Alex smiled at his uncle. "I guess it had to happen sooner or later."

"Yeah, I guess so. I hear you might volunteer for a twin study."

"We're thinking of it." So Tanner had been talking about something other than hockey with his uncle.

"It sounds fascinating. You might get written up in a paper or something."

"I think we'll find out what they're researching first."

Tanner was back outside a few minutes later. "Zoe's on her way over," he told Alex.

"She is?"

Tanner looked sheepish "She pretty much invited herself and I couldn't really think of any reason why she couldn't come."

"Somehow that doesn't surprise me."

Tanner glanced at Alex's uncle. "I hope that's okay with you, Uncle John."

"That's fine. But perhaps you'd better get dressed before she arrives."

Tanner looked down at the flannel shorts he'd slept in.

"Actually, Uncle John," Alex commented, "Zoe would probably prefer Tanner just the way he is."

"Shut up, Alex," Tanner yelled, running into the house.

Alex's uncle laughed. "This is great. Reminds me of the old times, when my own boys lived at home. I never thought I'd miss the bickering."

Alex looked at him, surprised. Yeah, maybe he had been an only child too long. He kind of enjoyed the bickering too. Bickering, yes. Fighting, no.

....

Alex let Zoe in the front door a few minutes later. She seemed to have grown about six inches. He looked down at her feet and noticed the platform sandals she was wearing. Her toenails had been painstakingly polished in a variety of patterns and a wide chain was strung around one ankle. When his eyes worked their way back up to meet hers, he was surprised to see the mischievous twinkle in them.

"Like them?" she asked, smiling.

"Oh yeah. They're great," he replied, not knowing whether she was referring to her toes, her shoes or her legs. Or perhaps it was the pair of butterflies she had tattooed onto her bare midriff. He wondered why he felt like a fool. He had to admit, though, there was something appealing about her. He sensed her crazy getups were just her way of poking fun at herself. This was a girl who didn't take life too seriously. A nice change, he thought.

"Where's Tanner?" she asked, stepping into the house.

"I'm Tanner," Alex pouted, pretending to be hurt that she didn't recognize him.

"You are not." She said it confidently, not at all unsure.

"Am too."

"Oh, okay," she teased. She grabbed his shoulders and planted a firm kiss on his cheek, which immediately turned crimson.

"Okay, okay, I'm not Tanner." He laughed as he stepped over to the hall mirror to check his reflection. He rubbed the lipstick smear on his skin. "How did you know?"

She studied him. "I'm not really sure. It's something about your eyes. Yours are ... sadder maybe. You don't look like you have too much fun."

"Really." Alex stared at the mirror. She was more perceptive than he had given her credit for. But he didn't like that description of himself. He would have to make a point of lightening up.

Tanner came down the hall just then. Zoe bounced up to him and threw her arms around his waist. Tanner gave her a quick squeeze and then gently pushed her away, glancing down the hall to see if Alex's uncle or mother had witnessed the hug.

"What do you guys want to do?" she asked.

"You guys?" asked Tanner. "You're including him in our plans?" Tanner used his thumb to indicate Alex, who was standing behind him.

"Sure, why not?" she asked. "He's kinda cute," she teased.

"Yeah, but he's an idiot," Tanner said.

"Takes one to know one," Alex said. "But don't worry, I have no intention of hanging out with you two anyway."

"I've got a babysitting job at three o'clock," Zoe told Tanner. "Why don't we walk down to the mall and get something to eat and just hang out until then?"

"Someone actually trusts you with their kids?" Alex asked.

She smiled back at him. "Oh, so you *do* have a sense of humor," she said. "Much better."

"I wasn't joking," Alex replied, but he grinned anyway.

She turned to Tanner. "Well?"

"I don't know ..."

Alex knew why he was hesitating. He was torn between going with Zoe or dealing with the e-mail messages he'd received the night before. "Go with Zoe," he suggested. "We'll hang out tonight."

Tanner nodded, understanding the implication. "Okay." He

pulled his runners out of the closet and wiggled his feet into them.

"Why don't you untie the laces?" Zoe asked.

"Too much trouble," Tanner replied, running his thumb around the back of the broken-down shoe so he could cram his heel into it. His hand felt his back pocket, checking for his wallet. "Let's go."

"Don't forget your house key," Alex cautioned, hoping Tanner would know that he was actually referring to the pepper spray.

"Got it," Tanner replied, patting his front pocket.

Alex watched them head down the sidewalk, Zoe taller than Tanner in her platform shoes. She draped her arm over Tanner's shoulder and leaned against him. Tanner glanced back at the house before putting his arm awkwardly around her waist. Zoe's laugh could be heard even after they'd rounded the corner.

Back in the house Alex went to the den, checked over his shoulder to make sure he was alone and then pulled the letter out of the drawer that he had stuffed it into late last night. He folded it carefully and pushed it into his pocket. Then he turned on the computer and waited for the e-mail messages to appear on the screen. There were no new ones, but he quickly deleted the one from their biological mother and printed the one from the university. He reread it and decided to take the matter into his own hands. He picked up the phone and dialed the number that was listed.

"Genetic Resource Center. Dr. Montgomery speaking."

"Hi. Yeah. I'm phoning about the twin study. I got your e-mail message."

"Oh, good. What's your name?" Alex noticed the sudden interest in the doctor's tone.

"Alex Swanson."

"And your twin's name?"

"Tanner Bolton."

There was a pause as the doctor jotted the names down. "You have different surnames."

"Yeah, we have different parents."

Another pause. "You are twins, though?"

"Yeah, but we were adopted by different families."

"At birth?"

"Yeah."

The voice became even more enthusiastic. "Really? And you're identical twins?"

"Yep."

"That's very exciting, Alex. There are so few monozygotic twins raised in different environments, but there is so much to learn from them."

"Monozygotic means identical?"

"Right. Sorry. I get carried away sometimes."

"That's okay. I'm phoning to get some more information about the study."

"Of course. What would you like to know?"

"First of all, how did you get our e-mail address?"

"Well, Alex, you've started with a tough one. I don't really know for sure. I have some student assistants that do the tracking down of twins for me. I don't know all their tricks, but it's amazing how much information is available on the Internet. It's scary, really, what people can find out about you."

"Oh, okay. Well, what do you do in your study?"

"Well, next week we're continuing our research on personality traits. We're trying to determine which traits are determined by our genes and which are shaped by the environment in which we are raised." He paused. "But you know, Alex, I didn't expect to hear from identical twins who were raised in different environments. Do you realize how important this is for twin research?"

"No, not really."

"It's *very* important. You see, identical twins share one hundred percent of their genes, but they usually grow up together, sharing a similar environment. When separated, it gives us clues about the strength of the genetic influence. If you are very alike in a particular trait — let's say you are both very stubborn — we expect that this trait is mainly influenced by your genes, but when you differ dramatically we expect that it is because of the environment you grew up in. Does that make sense?"

"Yeah, sort of." Alex could feel his mind whirling. He had wondered about this stuff just the other night. He felt himself drawn into the doctor's enthusiasm.

"My particular interest is that of the twin bond. One of our tests asks the twins to sit in different rooms and to draw whatever comes into their minds. I discovered, in one study, that twins often draw the same thing. However, when one was asked to draw an object and transmit that to the other twin, the results were disappointing. The conclusion of that study, then, was that it is not telepathy that's at work, but the fact that twins' thought patterns are so similar."

"You'd hoped that telepathy was involved? You actually believe in that stuff?"

"Well, of course I do. After all, family ties go far beyond physical presence."

"We'd like to do *that* study!"

"You would? How come?"

"Because I think we would change those conclusions."

"Really? You and your brother are telepathic?"

"Yeah, sort of. We can send images to each other."

The doctor's voice quivered with excitement. "Alex, I must meet you and your brother. Tell me a little more about yourselves."

"What do you want to know?"

"First of all, how old are you?"

"Fifteen."

"Oh. I'm glad I asked. I'll have to get your parents' consent to involve you in the study."

"Oh. All of our parents?"

"Yes. Is that a problem?"

Alex explained how Tanner's family lived in Edmonton, but the doctor said they could just fax a note of consent and Alex would only need a letter of consent from his mother.

"Now tell me, Alex, if you were separated at birth, how did you come to meet each other?"

Alex gave a brief account of their meeting last December.

"So it was your telepathy that brought you together?"

"Yeah, I guess you could say it was. And Tanner's dreams."

"What about his dreams?"

Alex explained how Tanner seemed to pick up Alex's troubles in his dreams and how he felt a trip to the coast would solve the mystery of them.

"Was Tanner's abduction written up in the newspapers?"

"Yeah, it was."

"You know, I vaguely recall reading about it. I'll bet that's what led my assistants to you. They're always on the lookout for new twin subjects."

Alex nodded. That made sense.

"Anyhow, I can't wait to meet you. This is just so exciting! Will you be able to get transportation to my clinic at UBC on Monday morning?"

"Yeah, I think so. But I'll let you know if there's a problem."

Alex smiled to himself when he hung up the phone. The doctor's enthusiasm was contagious. He decided to phone Caitlin and share the news.

"That's really cool, Alex," she said when he'd told her about his conversation with the doctor. "You guys may become famous!"

Alex laughed. "I wouldn't go that far. But it should be interesting."

"That's for sure."

"You want to go for a walk or something? Zoe came over this morning and abducted Tanner." Alex winced at his own words. He didn't know why he'd said that.

Caitlin laughed at the description. "She is pretty forceful, isn't she? Sure. Why don't I meet you at the playground in half an hour?"

Alex was feeling so good he decided to ignore his fear of going out alone. He put his key chain with the pepper spray in his pocket and left the house. His mind was whirling with thoughts of the twin study so he wasn't sure of the exact moment he sensed he was being followed, but when he circled back around the way he'd come and the man continued to follow him, his heart began to race. This could be the contact from Hap that he needed in order to plan his retaliation! He worked his way over to the park, carefully staying out in the open, and then sat on a bench, across the park from the playground. He didn't want to get Caitlin involved in this. Alex heard the man approaching from behind. He put his hand in his pocket and squeezed the vial. Suddenly the stranger was beside him. Without slowing his pace he dropped an envelope in Alex's lap and kept walking. Alex studied him as he went past but didn't think he'd seen him before. It was hard to be sure, though, because he had sunglasses and a cap on, but it was definitely a white male with a slim build. Alex watched as he left the park and then opened the envelope and pulled out a scrap of paper. All that was written on it was a phone number and the words "two o'clock." He looked at his watch. That was just twenty minutes away. He glanced across the park to the playground. He could see Caitlin heading toward the swings. He considered avoiding her and going straight to a phone, alone, but decided against it.

....

"What are you going to do?" she asked when he showed her the note and explained what had just happened.

"I'm going to find a phone and make the call. What did you think?"

"I don't think you should communicate with them."

"I have to. They've been stalking me and everyone I know and I'm sick of it. I need to know what they want."

"I think you're making a mistake."

"I'm sorry, Caitlin. But I've got to do it." He glanced at his watch. "And I've got to find a phone now."

Caitlin studied him for a moment, obviously trying to come to a decision. "I just live in the next block. No one's home. You can use my phone."

"Are you sure?"

She nodded, and they walked to her house in silence. At exactly two o'clock Alex picked up the phone in her kitchen and dialed. It only rang once.

"Alex." It was a female voice, and it was choked with emotion. "Don't testify, Alex."

"Who is this?"

"Maureen," she croaked. "Don't testify, Alex. They'll kill you."

"Where are you, Maureen?" Alex asked. He was so intent on hearing her answer that he didn't notice Caitlin quietly leave the room.

"It doesn't matter. I'm sorry, Alex, so sorry ..." The voice trailed off.

"Maureen? Maureen, are you there?"

"She's gone, Alex." It was a male voice. "And you'll be gone too if you don't heed her words."

"Who's this?"

"One more thing. Don't go to Russell. If you do, your pretty little friend, the one from the library, she goes too."

Alex heard the click as the person on the other end hung up. He replaced the phone in its cradle and glanced around the room, wondering where Caitlin had gone. She walked into the kitchen a moment later, carrying a portable phone. Her face was ashen.

.... fifteen

There was a spring in Tanner's step as he walked up the sidewalk toward Alex's uncle's home. He'd had a great afternoon with Zoe. First, they'd gone into a music store and she'd had him listen to songs with bizarre lyrics at one of the listening stations.

"People actually buy this stuff?" he'd asked her.

"Yup."

Tanner wondered what his mom would say if he played these CDs at home.

She'd hauled him into a woman's clothing store next, and had him pose as a mannequin so she could dress him in silly hats and costume jewelry. He'd tolerated her laughter for awhile, but when she began to wind boas and scarves around his neck he finally decided he'd had enough of being her toy. They'd sat on a bench in the mall then, and Zoe had scored the passing teens according to her "coolness" rating. He'd have a failing score, she'd said, with his undyed, gel-free hair and his lack of body rings or tattoos, but he noticed, with relief, that his low rating didn't seem to affect how she felt about him.

She'd been constantly touching or leaning against him, and when they ran into people that she knew, she'd put her arm possessively around him.

He jogged up the stairs and found the front door open. He burst in and hollered "Hello!" but the house was still. Everyone seemed to be out. He stepped into the kitchen and was shocked to see a strange man sitting at the kitchen table with a half-empty beer bottle on the table in front of him. Tanner recognized it as the brand Alex's uncle sometimes drank.

"Hi, Alex."

"It's Tanner. Who are you?"

The man pushed back his chair, stood up and walked toward Tanner. "Pack your bags, boy. We're going home."

"I beg your pardon?" Tanner recoiled from the smell of the man. Stale cigarette smoke mixed with alcohol. And body odor. Bad body odor. It must have been a week since this man had showered. So this was Alex's father, and, judging from the slur in his words and the way he swayed as he stood in front of him, he must have spent the afternoon in the bar before coming over here. "How did you get in?" Tanner asked.

"John hasn't moved the hidden house key in twenty years. Such a trusting guy. Anyway, you heard me, son. Pack your bags. We're going home. And where's your mother? She's coming with us."

Tanner knew better than to pick a fight with this man. He'd heard enough stories. But he wasn't sure how to proceed. Hadn't Mr. Swanson been told that Alex had met his brother and they were spending time together? He hadn't blinked an eye when he'd said he was Tanner. Didn't even seem to hear him. Tanner decided to go along with the game.

"Whatever you say, Dad. I'll give Mom a call. Tell her to get right on home."

Tanner saw the drunken man's eyes narrow. He'd obviously

expected a fight and was suspicious of Tanner's compliant attitude.

"Are you trying to trick me, Alex? You know I won't have any of that." He raised his arm and went to cuff the side of Tanner's head, but Tanner had plenty of time to prepare himself. He struck Mr. Swanson's arm away.

That did it. Mr. Swanson stared at Tanner, his eyes registering amazement, then rage. With an incoherent grunt, he flew at Tanner, taking him to the floor. Tanner was caught totally unprepared this time. He felt his shoulders slam against the floor and he struggled to keep his head from smashing. He was surprised the man had the strength or agility to knock him down. But Tanner was in good shape and, of course, sober, so was able to heave the flailing body off him and struggle to his feet. The phone was just within reach. He snatched it up and punched in 9-1-1 just as hands clamped around his throat, squeezing. He dropped the phone and stepped back onto his assailant's foot, crunching the toes as hard as he could. Mr. Swanson hollered but didn't relax his grip on Tanner's throat. If anything, he squeezed even harder in his pain and rage. The breath in Tanner's throat was hot, burning hot. It felt like a metal poker was jammed into his lungs. Tanner pried at the man's hands. Desperately, he jabbed his elbow in his attacker's stomach, but they were so close that it had no impact.

Blood was pounding in Tanner's head. Blindly, he pulled at a kitchen drawer, groping for a weapon, but Mr. Swanson yanked him away. He struggled to breathe. He felt like he might suffocate. He tried reaching over his head and was able to get a couple fistfuls of the man's hair, but it didn't have any effect on the strangling grip.

Tanner was losing strength. In a final effort to free himself he tried hooking his foot behind him and around his attacker's leg in order to trip him. But Mr. Swanson seemed to have sobered up enough to maintain his balance. Then, just as the world went black, Tanner heard a decorative plate smash on the floor. Then another. And another.

"What the …"

A plate smashed by their feet. Tanner felt the man jolt, startled. And the fingers loosened. Not much. But enough. Choking in a breath, Tanner lunged backward, forcing Mr. Swanson to step back to maintain his balance, and as he did his foot crunched onto the shards from the plates and he slipped and fell heavily to the floor, releasing his grip as he went down. Tanner grabbed a carving knife out of the wooden block that stood on the counter.

"Don't move!" he rasped, pointing the knife at the man sprawled among the broken china. The knife felt heavy in his hand, and he struggled to keep from shaking. The man cursed, and rolled up on one elbow.

He tried to kill me, Tanner thought. This drunken excuse for a man had tried to kill him.

Mr. Swanson glared at Tanner from bloodshot eyes. He pushed himself up a little further.

The knife felt sure now, his breath less ragged. Tanner would do whatever he needed to — if the man tried anything else.

Mr. Swanson began to sit up.

"Don't even think about it," Tanner said.

The one remaining plate on the wall fell and smashed on the floor. Sirens sounded in the distance.

.... sixteen

"What does he mean by 'goes'? She *goes* too?"

"It's just big-shot talk, Caitlin. Don't worry." Once again, Alex was amazed at how easily he could lie.

"Who's Russell?"

"He's a police officer. Officer Russell. He's not in charge of our case, but he's taken a special interest in it. In us, actually."

"Phone him."

"What?"

"I said phone him. Right now."

"Caitlin, are you crazy? You heard what he said."

"Yeah, but you said it was just big-shot talk."

"Well, it is but …"

"But what, Alex?"

Alex studied his hands, stumped. How could he reassure her when he knew exactly what these guys could do? His failure to answer must have confirmed her fears. Looking up as she slumped into a chair, he could see that she knew it wasn't just talk.

He wasn't such a good liar after all.

"What have you got me into, Alex?" she whispered, rubbing the goosebumps that had surfaced on her arms despite the heat of the summer day.

"I'm sorry, Caitlin," he said quietly, clearing his throat. "I never meant to get you involved." Or Tanner, he thought, or anyone else.

There was a long silence. Finally, Caitlin spoke. "So, what are we going to do now?"

"We?"

She shrugged. "We have to do something. Just wishing I'd never met you isn't going to solve anything."

Alex tried to laugh, but it came out as more of a snort. "The other night you had me convinced that you were a chicken."

"I still am." Alex heard the tremble in her voice. "But I'm trying to change, remember?"

Alex reached across the table and gently touched her hand. He decided to confide in her. "I have a plan — sort of. But even Tanner doesn't know about it yet."

She pulled her hand away. "What is it?"

Alex's eyes narrowed. "Actually, discovering that Maureen is still alive was crucial. Now I know exactly what I have to do next."

"Which is?"

"Rescue her."

"You're not serious."

"Yeah, I am." The plan began to gel even more clearly as he spoke. "Maureen's being held hostage because of us — Tanner and I; Tanner almost got killed because of me and Hap's responsible for all of that. I have to make him pay."

"What are you getting at?"

"The only sure way to get him convicted is for all three of us to testify."

"Okay, but how are you going to figure out where she is?"

Alex thought about that. His original plan was to set up a kind of sting operation — with the police. But now it was clear that they couldn't possibly get the police involved. But if Caitlin was willing to help, and maybe Zoe ...

"I still have to fine-tune the details, Caitlin, but it might mean I have to get myself abducted, just temporarily."

"Temporarily! What are you talking about?"

"I know it sounds dangerous, but it's like this. Once I find Maureen I can contact Tanner and he'll lead the police to us."

"Contact Tanner? You think they're going to let you pick up the phone and call him?"

Alex smiled. "No. I'm not quite that stupid."

"No? This plan sounds pretty stupid to me."

He ignored her comment. "Remember I told you how we first met through our telepathy?"

"Yeah."

"Well, it worked then. It can work again."

"Alex, you're nuts. A million, no, a billion things could go wrong. They could kill you before you've even made contact with Tanner."

"They could, but I don't think they will. They haven't killed Maureen yet, right? I'm sure they plan to when they're finished with her, but so far they haven't. They needed her to talk to me. And they'll need me to get to Tanner."

"Alex, you're making this sound like a game. It's not. Those guys are dangerous. You may think you'll come out looking like a ..." She paused. "Like some kind of hero, but it's way more likely that you'll come out dead."

"Believe me, Caitlin," he said, a hint of anger in his voice. "I know better than anybody how dangerous these guys are. And I'm not doing this to look like a hero. I'm doing it because I owe it to Tanner and Maureen."

"Whatever. But it's still a bad idea."

"Have you got a better one?"

She shook her head. "You know I don't."

"Listen, Caitlin. I'll talk to Tanner about this tonight. I don't think Hap realizes that we're being subpoenaed, but when he finds out he'll know that we *have* to testify, and then he'll think he has no choice but to kill us. But my abduction has to be on my terms. Do you know what I mean?"

"No."

"Well, first of all, Tanner and I can't both get nabbed at the same time. It has to be just me."

"I don't like this at all, Alex."

"Listen, Caitlin, you'll be fine as long as you don't contact Officer Russell, just like they said. All right?"

Caitlin looked resigned. "Fine."

"I better go. Are you going to be okay?"

She glanced at her watch and nodded. "My parents will be home any minute."

"Good. I'll phone you later."

....

Alex found himself constantly looking over his shoulder on his way home and wished he had his cousin's bike to get him there faster. All the talk about abduction had definitely unnerved him. He stuffed his hand in his pocket and clutched the vial of pepper spray. As he hustled through the park, he suddenly felt his throat constrict, bringing him to an abrupt halt. What was happening? He bent over at the waist, his hands on his knees, wheezing, gasping for air. He couldn't breathe! He began to panic.

Then, just as abruptly, the sensation passed, but not the panic.

He took a deep breath and stood up. What was he picking up? Had something happened to Tanner? He began to run, acutely aware of sirens wailing in the distance. A few minutes later he rounded the corner that led to his uncle's home and was shocked to see the flashing lights of a police car and an ambulance, both parked right outside the house.

Was he too late? Had they done something to someone in his family already? He raced down the street, up the steps and practically crashed into two police officers coming out the front door. His father, cursing and handcuffed, struggled between them. He stopped short when he came face to face with Alex.

"Alex?"

"Dad! What are *you* doing here?"

His father looked completely baffled. They stared at each other while the police officers looked from one to the other.

Finally, one of them broke the silence. "This is your father?"

"Yes." He fought back the urge to add "unfortunately."

"Then I think we have some talking to do." He turned to Alex's dad. "Do you think you can control yourself if we go back inside and try to straighten things out?"

Mr. Swanson nodded but continued to stare mutely at Alex.

As they turned to go back inside, Alex saw Tanner standing just inside the screen door with a paramedic beside him. The puzzle pieces began to fit together.

They sat at the kitchen table, Alex and Tanner on one side, and Mr. Swanson, with the two officers flanking him, on the other. Tanner had insisted that he wasn't seriously injured so the paramedics had left in the ambulance. Alex was shocked at the mess in the kitchen. The floor was covered in broken plates. He glanced at Tanner, who was pale and sullen.

One of the officers noticed Alex's worried glance. He turned to Tanner. "You're sure you're okay?"

Tanner just nodded. Alex noticed how red his neck was, especially compared to his sheet-white face. His father had done something awful to him, and it was his fault, again.

"Now let's get the story straight, Mr. Swanson," began one of the officers. "You said you came to take your son home, your runaway son, and that he attacked you when you told him to pack his bag."

Mr. Swanson didn't answer. He just looked from one boy to the other.

"Are both these boys your sons, sir? They certainly look alike."

He shook his head.

The officer raised his eyebrows. "No? Then which one is?"

Mr. Swanson didn't say anything. Alex answered for him. "I am."

"But this must be your twin brother," the officer said, pointing to Tanner.

"Yes, but we were adopted by two different families. This is my dad. Tanner's lives in Edmonton."

The other officer suddenly sat up. "I remember you two. One of you was abducted last winter, and there was some confusion as to who was who."

"That was us," Alex replied.

"Let's see if I have this straight," continued the first officer, addressing Mr. Swanson. "Alex is the runaway son that you — and I quote — 'simply came to take home where he belongs'."

Alex heard the sarcasm, loud and clear.

Mr. Swanson nodded. He stared at Tanner.

"And you must have mistaken Tanner for your own son."

He nodded again.

"You'd not met Tanner before?"

He shook his head.

The officer turned to Alex again. "Your father claimed, quite adamantly, I might add, that you were a runaway and that you needed to go home."

"I live here with my mother and my uncle. My mom is filing for divorce."

"Oh," said the officer. "That sheds quite a different light on the story." He looked at Tanner. "And you came home and were attacked by this man, a complete stranger to you."

"I figured out who he was."

Alex cringed at the rasp in Tanner's voice.

"Did you try to explain who you were?"

"I tried, but he wasn't listening."

Mr. Swanson suddenly jumped to his feet. "How the hell was I supposed to know you weren't Alex!"

The officer pulled him back down, but Alex felt himself cringe. He'd almost forgotten how much his father's rages affected him.

"I think, sir," said the officer, "that we need to take you down to the station until you've calmed down."

Mr. Swanson erupted again. " I refuse to say another thing until I've talked to my lawyer!" he hollered. "I haven't been read my rights!"

The officers dragged him down to the car, where he was pushed into the back seat and handcuffed to the door. A stream of obscenities spewed from his mouth, mostly directed at the officers but with the odd reference to the boys too. One officer climbed into the vehicle and made a call on his radio while the other one came back up the stairs to talk to the brothers, who were standing there quietly, watching.

"I suggest that your mother get a restraining order placed on him," he said to Alex. Then he turned to Tanner. "And we'll charge him with assault and battery if you like."

Tanner glanced at Alex and shook his head.

"It's up to you," the officer said, jogging back down the stairs.

"Go for it," said Alex.

"I'd like to," Tanner replied. "Believe me. But," he sighed, "he is your father, and he is still your mom's husband, for now. And there's enough stuff going on with your family without adding that to it."

Alex nodded, feeling extremely weary. Yeah, he thought to himself, there was.

....

The brothers swept up the mess in the kitchen and then flopped onto their beds, exhausted.

"Your dad's even worse than I'd imagined."

Alex shook his head, still shocked by the description Tanner had given him of his dad's attack. "The last six months certainly haven't improved him any."

"I'm surprised you didn't run away years ago."

"It's hard when you're little. You don't know any better. And besides," Alex mused, "I don't think he used to be so bad."

"Maybe our birth mom will take you in. You deserve a decent family."

Alex spoke sharply. "I love my mom, Tanner. A lot. And I've got my uncle. I don't need another family."

"Yeah, well, it's not fair. It's not your fault you were adopted and given to him."

"Haven't you heard, Tanner? Life's not fair."

They lay quietly on their beds for a few minutes, a chasm of unspoken thoughts hanging in the air between them. At the mention of the words "birth mom" Alex had remembered that Tanner was probably planning his response to the message he'd received last night. But Alex had stuff he wanted to talk about too.

"Hap contacted me again today."

"Yeah?" Tanner rolled onto his side and propped himself up with his elbow. "What happened?"

Alex told his brother about the man who'd followed him, the envelope that was dropped in his lap and, finally, about the phone call he'd made.

"So she's still alive."

"Yeah."

"What are we going to do?"

Alex noticed that Tanner had said "we", not "you". Caitlin had said the same thing.

"Well, we're not going to go to the cops. But I do have a plan."

"Which is?"

Alex took a deep breath and then answered, the words coming out with a rush of air. "I'm going to get myself abducted so I can find out where Maureen is, and then you're going to bring help to the location that I send to you."

A tiny smile tugged at the corners of Tanner's mouth. "You're kidding, right?"

"Wrong."

Tanner sat up. "No way!"

"Way."

The kitchen door, on the other side of the house, banged open. "Hello, boys!" hollered Alex's mom. "We're home. Come and ..." There was a brief pause and then she continued. "Alex! Where are you!"

"Coming, Mom!" Alex turned to his brother. "You stay here. I'll say you're resting."

Tanner lay back down on his cot. "Actually, I am tired. Sending those plates off the wall was a major energy drain. Call me if you need me."

"Okay. We'll talk later."

"You can be sure of that."

Alex noticed that Tanner's eyes were closed already. It had been quite a day. And it wasn't over yet.

seventeen

Tanner lay on his cot with his eyes closed, but he didn't fall asleep. His mind was jumbled with thoughts of Alex's father and the horrible memory of those strong hands gripping his neck, squeezing … Fortunately, Mr. Swanson hadn't moved from the floor while they'd waited for the police to arrive. It had only taken them two or three minutes to get there, but it felt like twenty to Tanner as he sweated it out, the knife clenched in his hand. If Alex's dad had moved, Tanner wondered, would he really have been able to use it? He swallowed hard. He almost wished he'd had the chance.

Tanner's eyes popped open. He had met only one other man as mean and violent as Alex's dad, and that was Hap. How ironic that Alex had run away from one only to end up dealing with the other. And now his life, too, was tangled up with them. But then, wasn't it because of those two men that he and Alex had met? Would he prefer to go back to the way it was — not even knowing he had a twin brother?

No. Meeting Alex had filled a huge void in his life. And now meeting his birth mom would fill another.

Tanner sat up. He probably should press charges. Why should Alex's dad get off the hook for attempted murder? That's what it was, wasn't it? He shook his head. He couldn't do it. He couldn't add more stress to his brother's already complicated life.

Leaning against the cool bedroom wall he could hear the murmur of voices coming from the kitchen. Had Alex ever had fantasies of killing his father? He wouldn't blame him if he had. Imagine enduring all those years of being treated like that. It wasn't fair. He didn't care what Alex said. He deserved better than that. Maybe, just maybe, their birth mother would be the ticket to Alex's future happiness.

Their birth mother! He hadn't replied to her letter yet. He got up and quietly opened the bedroom door. Voices could still be heard coming from down the hall. Silently, he crept to the den and closed the door behind him. He turned on the computer and clicked on the icon for the Internet. He massaged his throat while he waited for the computer to dial it up.

There was another letter from her! He quickly scrolled down.

Dear Son,

I've been watching the Findme site all day, hoping to hear from you. Have you changed your mind? What is the problem?

YBM

Short and to the point, Tanner thought. Bordering on rude, actually. She must really be anxious to hear from them. He scrolled up to reread yesterday's message, but it was gone. Alex had worked fast. He pointed the mouse at the Bookmarks icon and clicked on the Findme site. He typed in his password and stared at the screen. What do you say to a mother you've never met? Dear Mom? No, it was too soon for that. He put his fingers on the keys and began to type.

Hi,

It's me. No, I haven't changed my mind but I was shocked to find you so quickly. I've only been searching for one week and I'm nervous, I guess, but excited too.

Yes, I'd like to meet you. Alex, my brother (and your other son), is even more nervous than me, but he'll get over it.

Where and when do you want to meet?

YBS

PS I've had a good life, so far, just in case you're wondering. My adoptive parents are great. Alex wasn't so lucky with his dad, but his mom's nice.

He reread what he'd written. It would have to do.

.... eighteen

"What's happened in here?" Alex's mother stared wide-eyed at the bare walls where the plates had hung. His uncle stood in the doorway, mouth gaping slightly, grocery bags tugging at his arms as he too looked around at the empty walls.

Alex shook his head sadly. He took the grocery bags from his mother's hands. "Dad dropped by this afternoon."

Startled, Alex's uncle and mom said nothing, just stared at Alex, waiting for him to continue.

"He let himself in, said he remembered where Uncle John kept the key. I was out too. Tanner was the first one home. He thought Tanner was me."

Alex paused, waiting for a response, but the adults just continued staring at him.

"He got into a fight with Tanner, choked him pretty bad. Tanner managed to call 9-1-1, though, and the police got here before they killed each other."

Mr. Bradshaw filled the kettle during the silence that followed. "Where's Tanner now, Alex?"

"He's in our room, resting."

"Is he okay?"

"I think so. The paramedics came, looked him over and left."

"Where's your dad?" Alex's mom looked pale, but less distraught than Alex had thought she would be. She sank into a chair.

"The police took him away. He was in one of his really ugly moods. They said something about putting a restraining order on him and that ... that you should call the station and they'd tell you all about it."

His mom nodded and accepted a cup of tea from his uncle.

"The plates came down when Tanner and Dad were fighting."

"That psychokinesis thing again?" asked his uncle.

Alex nodded. "Sorry."

Mr. Bradshaw poured himself some tea and they all sat at the kitchen table. No one spoke for a moment. "That was your aunt's collection," Alex's uncle said finally. "She loved those plates — each one held a special memory for her. I left them there because they reminded me of her."

The three of them sat quietly, thinking of Mr. Bradshaw's late wife.

Alex's mom was the first to speak. She put her hand on her brother's. "I'm sorry, John. We've brought our troubles into your life."

Alex's uncle covered her hand with his own. "We're family, Pat. We stick together. We knew he'd show up one day. I'm just surprised it took this long."

Mrs. Swanson only nodded.

....

Later, as they lay in bed, Alex told Tanner about his phone conversation with Dr. Montgomery.

"I wish you could have heard him when I explained that we were identical twins separated at birth."

Tanner's eyebrows rose.

"He can't wait to get us into his lab. He figures he'll learn a lot from us, something about whether our environment or our genes shaped our personalities."

"Jeans?"

"Genes." Alex spelled it out. "G-E-N-E-S. Like DNA and all that."

"Oh, those genes." Tanner smiled. "So you said we'd do the study?"

"Yeah, I hope that's okay with you."

Tanner nodded.

"And get this. His own pet interest is in the twin bond. He wants to test our telepathy."

"Yeah?"

"Apparently it's not something other twins can do effectively."

"He's in for a surprise."

"I told him we were pretty talented in that area, but it's probably something you've got to see to believe." As Alex watched Tanner rub his throat he recalled his own sensation of choking that afternoon, on his way home from Caitlin's. "You know, I think I'm picking up on your problems now too, sort of like the way you've always picked up on mine."

"What did you pick up?"

"I felt something squeezing my throat this afternoon and I felt faint, too. It must have happened at the same time my dad was choking you."

"Lucky you. Maybe this doctor can help us learn how to quit sending the messages."

"Or have more control over them," Alex suggested. "Actually, we're going to need as much control as we can get for my abduction."

"You're really serious about that?"

"Yep."

Tanner shook his head. "What if something screws up?"

"It can't."

"Why not?"

"I won't let it."

"They may not kill you right away, Alex, but they could torture you pretty bad."

"We won't give them time."

Tanner shook his head. "You're nuts, Alex. This is way too dangerous!"

"I'm not excited about your plans either, Tanner."

"That reminds me. I replied to her note this afternoon."

"You did? I've got her letter in my pocket."

"She sent another one."

"What did you say?"

"I said we'd meet her. That it's up to her to name a place and suggest a time."

"How do you know she lives in Vancouver?"

Tanner shrugged. "I just assumed she did."

Alex yawned and pulled the sheet over his shoulder. "What a day. Did you check the window? Is it locked?"

"Yeah, though I'm beginning to wonder if abduction is preferable to suffocation. It gets so hot in here."

"Leave the hall door open."

Tanner got up and opened it. He glanced at his brother's tired face. "And don't send me any nightmares tonight."

"Not much I can do about that." Alex switched off his reading light and turned over. "Unless you sleep during the day and I sleep at night."

Tanner continued to flip through one of his books. "Very funny. Maybe *you* could sleep during the day."

As it turned out, Alex worried needlessly about creating nightmares for his brother. A person has to be sleeping to have dreams, and with their minds so full of their surreptitious plans, neither twin slept much that night.

.... nineteen

A strange sight awaited Tanner and Alex on Monday morning when they walked into Dr. Montgomery's office carrying their parent-signed letters of consent. The reception area was jammed with people, people of all ages, sizes and skin colors. But the strange part was, there was two of everyone.

"Kinda reminds you of Noah's ark, doesn't it?" Tanner mumbled to Alex.

"Huh?" Alex looked at Tanner, puzzled.

"You know, two of every species."

Alex groaned. "Shut up, Tanner."

A man in a white lab coat suddenly burst into the room. His assistants, each in identical lab coats, followed him. Tanner couldn't help thinking how out of place they each looked without a matching partner.

"Welcome, twins," the older man said. "For those of you new to this study, I'm Dr. Montgomery, and this," he motioned to the group assembled behind him, "is my team, who will be working with us this week. We'd like to thank you in advance for participating in our research and for helping us try to shed more light on the age-old nature-versus-nurture debate, the one that asks whether it is our environment or our genetic make–up that most influences our personality." He pulled off his glasses as he spoke and carefully cleaned each lens with the handkerchief he kept in his breast pocket. "It is widely believed that it is a combination of both components that determines who we are, but we are still trying to establish which personality traits are more strongly influenced by which component."

Tanner sighed. How long was this guy going to babble on? He glanced at Alex and was surprised to see how attentively he was listening to the man's ramblings.

"This is very important research that you have committed to," the doctor continued, "because our findings could implement social change in this country. For example, if it is proven that it is mainly environmental influences that determine intelligence, then it would be important that good preschool education programs are available to all children to ensure stimulating intellectual development.

"Each of you is unique, even if it doesn't look that way," he said, smiling as a chuckle rumbled through the twin subjects, "and it is the differences between you that I mostly want to focus on this week.

"You will be asked to do a number of tasks over the next five days, some with your twin and some without. You will start apart today, answering questions on a survey, and then you will be reunited with your twin later this morning to discuss your answers with a member of my team. My assistants will make notes about your discussion, keeping track of the differences in your personality traits."

Tanner had a perfect example of a personality trait he and Alex didn't share: their sense of humor. Alex was far too morose. He'd have to point that out to the researchers.

"Any questions?" asked the doctor finally.

Seeing none, the doctor distributed the survey sheets and directed the twins into two different rooms. Tanner found a chair and was just about to look over the questionnaire when he felt a tap on his shoulder.

"Are you Tanner?" asked one of the lab-coated assistants.

"Yes."

"The doctor would like to see you in his office. It's just down the hall, on the left. His name's on the door. You can't miss it."

When Tanner entered the doctor's office, he found Alex already seated there.

"Hello, Tanner," said the doctor, stretching out his hand to shake Tanner's. "So glad to meet you. Please come in and have a seat."

Tanner sat next to Alex and the doctor sat in the chair behind his desk. He did not look like the scholarly researcher Tanner had expected to meet, but more like a mad scientist with his unruly gray hair and checkered pants that stuck out below his lab coat. And he was obviously very pleased to meet them — his grin was huge and his eyes shone.

"Forgive me, boys, for staring, but you have no idea how delighted I am you've decided to take part in my research. Studying twins has been my life's work but I've met very few sets of identical siblings who were reared separately. You have the potential to offer so much to my findings."

Tanner nodded, smiled and glanced at Alex. Alex was looking more relaxed and cheerful than he'd seen him in days.

"I'll be working specifically with you two this week, and we'll be doing somewhat different tasks than the other sets of twins. There is so much more I can learn from you, and really, I'm just so delighted to have this opportunity to get to know you." He sat back in his chair and stared at the boys once more, shaking his head slightly and grinning as though he'd just drawn the winning numbers in a million-dollar lottery.

Tanner felt himself blush slightly. To hide his awkwardness he glanced down at the survey sheet he was still holding and read a few of the subtitles in the left-hand margin: *Impulsiveness, Response to Strangers, Friendliness, Task Persistence*. Beside each personality trait there were hypothetical situations and you had to rate yourself, on a scale of one to ten, as to how closely your response matched the one in the example.

"You can hand those sheets over to me, boys," the doctor said, reaching across his desk to collect them. "We might get around to them later, but right now I'd really like to hear more about this twin bond that Alex said you two shared. Can you tell me about it?"

Tanner glanced at Alex, who shrugged his shoulders before answering. "I think I told you everything about it on the phone the other day."

"Okay then, you said you were telepathic. Can you demonstrate it for me?"

"Sure." Tanner stood up, eager to show off a little. "I'll go into the corridor, you suggest something for Alex to focus on, and when I receive it I'll come and tell you what it is."

"Perfect."

Tanner stepped into the hallway and waited, closing his eyes and trying to make his mind go blank. Within seconds he saw a beautiful waterfall cascading down a mountain. He stepped back into the room.

"I saw a waterfall."

The doctor smacked his desk and smiled his lottery-winning smile again. "That's awesome. Let's do it again. Alex, you go in the hallway this time."

As soon as Alex stepped out of the room, closing the door behind him, the doctor whispered, "Send him a hippopotamus." Tanner did as he was told and Alex came back a moment later.

"A hippopotamus."

"Right on," exclaimed the doctor. "That's the most remarkable thing I've seen in a long time. Can you read each other's thoughts and secrets too?"

The boys shook their heads in unison. Tanner spoke up. "No. It's always an object or picture that we have to focus on and actually 'push' out. Push is the only word I can think of to describe it, but without the push the other guy doesn't pick anything up."

"That's very interesting." He jotted something on his pad of paper and then looked at Tanner. "Alex said something about you picking up his stress in your dreams."

"Yeah, that's something else we do, although we'd rather not. We also have telekinesis — we make things move when we're really pissed off about something."

"Really. Can you demonstrate that?"

The boys glanced at each other again. Tanner answered. "We could, but we don't like to." He sighed. "You see, first we have to get ..." He paused, trying to think of the best word. "We have to get enraged about something and then we have no control over what is going to move. And the worst part is, it totally wipes you out. It's another so-called *talent* we'd like to get rid of."

"Hmm." The doctor appeared lost in thought, although his pencil kept tapping the pad of paper.

"How many people know about these talents of yours?"

"Not too many," Tanner answered. "Last winter we had to tell the police how Alex knew I was under the Lions Gate Bridge, but I don't think they really believed us. Alex's mom and uncle know about the telekinesis, but they don't say too much about it. We figured if we told people we would have to demonstrate it all the time and we really don't want to. It makes us feel like freaks."

"Good plan," said the doctor, still looking distracted. "If the media got a hold of you two, there's no saying what could happen. Things could get out of hand, fast."

The doctor sat staring at the boys, serious now, pencil still tapping the pad. "I'm in a quandary," he said finally. "I can't decide exactly what to do with you boys now that I have you. It's imperative that I proceed with the nature-versus-nurture research but I'm very tempted to explore these other talents you share first." He stared at the boys some more. "What are your plans for the rest of the summer?"

"I'm going home on Sunday," Tanner answered.

"And I'm back to work next Monday."

"Oh, no. I can't believe it!" The doctor got up and began pacing around his office. "I need much more than a week with you." He went back to his desk and fell into his chair. His pencil tapping became more furious as he considered the situation. "Listen, boys. I'm going to apply for some exigency funding for this research. If I can get it, is there any way you can prolong your vacation here, Tanner?"

"Maybe." Tanner felt his heart start to race. He'd been trying to figure out how to get his trip extended so he would have more time to get to know his birth mom if the initial reunion went well. "My parents wanted me to come camping with them, but they might let me stay on. They're pretty big on scientific stuff and this kinda falls into that category." He glanced at Alex. "If Alex's uncle will let me stay, that is."

"We'll assume he will," the doctor said. "We have to think positively. What kind of a job do you have, Alex?"

"I work at the airport, cleaning planes."

"It's a summer job? You're just trying to earn some cash or ...?"

"No, I don't plan to make a career of it, if that's what you're asking," Alex laughed. "I'm just summer relief."

"If I get this exigency funding, then, and could match your salary, would you quit your job and spend the time here instead?"

"I think that would be okay." He paused, then continued, thinking out loud, " My uncle got me the job, but, like Tanner said, he'll probably appreciate the fact that this is educational." He hesitated again, then added with a smile, "My boss will be ticked but he'll get over it. Anyone can clean planes."

Tanner cleared his throat. "Would I get paid too?"

The doctor winked. "Maybe I'll pay Alex's uncle your room and board."

"That sucks."

The doctor laughed. "Let's see if I actually get the funding and then we'll quibble, okay Tanner? But remember. Think positively. I need you guys."

....

In the car driving home that afternoon the boys told Alex's uncle about their day, including the doctor's plans to apply for exigency funding to keep them on. They waited quietly for his response.

"I think it's a good idea," he said finally, after driving some distance in silence. "Perhaps something useful will come from you two being separated after all."

"You don't mind if I stay with you a little longer, then?" Tanner asked.

"You're welcome to stay as long as you like, Tanner. Regardless of whether you're involved in the study or not." Alex's uncle cleared his throat. "You boys belong together. Always have, in my mind."

"Thank you." Alex's dad may be a total jerk, Tanner thought, but his uncle was cool.

"You still haven't talked to Alex's mom about your search, though, have you, Tanner?"

"No." He slumped a little in his seat.

"Are you still planning to conduct one?"

"Yes." Planning to conduct one? What would he say if he knew he'd already contacted her!

"Then you better get onto it."

They weren't going to tell Alex's mom now. It was too late. He slouched a little lower in his seat, avoiding eye contact with Alex, who he knew was staring at him, wondering if he was going to confess. He didn't say anything, but stared out the window quietly.

Alex changed the subject. "I wonder why we haven't received the subpoena to testify at the trial yet. It was last week that Officer Russell told us about it."

"There's a lot of red tape involved in these legal things," his uncle said.

"I suppose, but it didn't take them long to get a restraining order placed on Dad."

"You're right." Mr. Bradshaw considered Alex's comment. "They made it sound like once they had your mom's consent, it was all taken care of." He glanced at his nephew. "Perhaps we should call them again tonight and just get these matters clarified for you."

"That's okay, Uncle John," Alex assured him, somewhat too enthusiastically, Tanner thought. "I was just wondering. It's no big deal."

Tanner went into the den and shut the door as soon as he got home. He turned on the computer and immediately dialed up the Internet. Sure enough, a message was waiting for him. He pressed the key to print it and then read it over quickly. As soon as it was printed he deleted the message.

It was confirmed. He was going to meet his mother.

.... twenty

Alex sighed when Tanner came barreling into their room clutch-ing a sheet of paper. It could only mean one thing.

"She wants to meet with us!"

"Does she say where and when?"

"Yep. Playland, next Saturday."

"Where in Playland?"

"Under the old roller coaster, at noon. Do you know where that is?"

Alex nodded. He flopped onto his bed. "I'm still not real excited about this, Tanner."

"Why not? What's the harm in it? We're not hurting any-one. We have a right to know who she is and where we came from."

"Are you sure you don't just want to do this alone?"

"Quit whining, Alex. She gave birth to twins, and now, fifteen years later, she's going to meet them. Don't you get a rush just thinking about it?"

"No, I get the creeps. We shouldn't be doing it."

"This gives you the creeps, yet you're planning to get yourself abducted? You're weird."

Yeah, maybe he was, Alex thought. But he had learned to trust his instincts over the past six months, and his instincts told him that something was not quite right here. He didn't know what, exactly, but he did know that he had only four days to talk Tanner out of it.

....

Tuesday and Wednesday came and went but the subpoena never arrived. Alex became anxious waiting for it. Once Hap knew that they *had* to testify, he'd make his plans to get rid of them, forcing Alex to put his own plan into place.

The work with Dr. Montgomery was intense, mentally draining, in fact, but the doctor's enthusiasm was so contagious that Alex looked forward to the sessions with him. They spent the mornings working on the nature/nurture research and the afternoons were devoted to exploring the parameters of their psychic abilities.

It was during the morning session on Thursday that the doctor helped him tap into some long forgotten memories of his childhood. The older man had taken their family histories and had then put the boys into an almost hypnotic trance. They were to try to recall and then describe their early years. Alex's thoughts had been transported to a long forgotten afternoon when he was only about three or four years old. It was a hot summer day and he was on the beach with his father, who was patiently teaching him to skip stones over the water. He remembered his dad showing him how to choose flat, round stones. Then he remembered how he'd held Alex's small fist in his own and had shown him how to fling the stone parallel with the water. When Alex grew tired of the game, his father had heaved him up onto his shoulders and carried him to the town's coffee shop, where he bought him a bright blue, bubble-gum-flavored ice-cream cone before they walked home together, hand in hand. He remembered another occasion too, when he was just a little older. It must have been fall because he and his dad were snuggling on the couch, fire blazing, watching football on TV. To this day Alex disliked TV sports, but he remembered he had so badly wanted to please his dad that he'd imitated everything he did. When his dad whooped over a good play, Alex whooped too. If his dad groaned, Alex groaned, even though he had no idea what he was groaning about. They laughed together at the commotion they were making. The memories reminded Alex that his father hadn't always been an angry, hostile man. The personality change had happened slowly, but it had been complete.

"Something wrong, Alex?" the doctor asked when Tanner left for a moment to use the washroom.

Alex nodded, though he was unsure why he felt so depressed after reliving such happy memories. "I guess it's just that I had forgotten the good times," he answered honestly. "All I remembered, until right now, was what a jerk Dad was."

"And that makes you sad?"

"Well, yeah. I realize now that it didn't have to be that way."

"Alcohol does change a person, that's for sure. Most people can handle it in moderation, but for people like your dad, it brings out the meanness in them, and yet, for some reason, they become addicted anyway."

"I always thought he didn't like me. You should have seen how he treated me."

"And how was that?"

"Well, aside from smacking me around, he never paid me for working in his gas station."

"But Alex, you said your father was European. Where he was raised, everyone worked together to run a family business. There was no expectation of being paid."

"Times have changed."

"That's true, and I don't condone the abuse, but it sounds like he's still very much 'old country'. He was raising you as he was raised himself. It's the way most people raise their children."

"Not me. I'll treat my kids like my uncle treats us — with respect."

The doctor nodded. "You can consciously model your own behavior after him. You're lucky. Most people only experience one style — that of their parents."

Alex closed his eyes and let himself slide back to the fuzzy comfort that the memories had created. His dad *had* loved him when he was little. When did that all change? And why?

....

That afternoon the boys were alone in Dr. Montgomery's office, exploring ways to block their psychic transmissions.

"Did you get that one?" Tanner asked.

"Nope," Alex answered, pleased with himself. "Blocked you again."

"Damn! Try sending me one."

Alex watched as Tanner closed his eyes and then he visualized a girl who looked as similar to Zoe as he could manage, dressed in the skimpiest of bathing suits. He pushed.

"Hey!" Tanner said. "That's not fair. How can I block a vision like that?"

"Face it, lover-boy. I'm the only one who can block. I've got it, you haven't!"

Tanner opened his mouth to disagree but Dr. Montgomery burst into the room just then, his professional demeanor completely gone as he smacked the boys on the back and danced about the room.

"We got it!" he announced, waving a sheet of paper in the air. "We got the funding! Alex will get paid equivalent to what he was making at the airport and Tanner will continue to make one hundred dollars a week. There is also money to reimburse Alex's uncle for Tanner's room and board."

Alex glanced at Tanner, eyebrows raised. The doctor spotted the look that passed between his two subjects and stopped dancing. He sat down behind his desk.

"Sorry, boys," he panted, sheepishly now. "I get carried away sometimes."

They sat quietly for a few minutes, smiling at each other. Now they had what Alex had been afraid to hope for before. It had taken a lot of skillful arguing, but Tanner had eventually worn his parents down and had their permission to stay for the remainder of the summer, and he himself was delighted to give up his cleaning job to become a research guinea pig.

The doctor was still grinning, looking almost smug now. There was no doubt about why he was so pleased. He was as obsessed with his research, Alex thought, as Tanner was with meeting their birth mom. And now Tanner would have the rest of the summer to get acquainted with her. Maybe. As long as Alex's own plan went smoothly. And he didn't dare consider the consequences if it didn't.

....

A police car sat waiting outside the house when they arrived home Friday afternoon. "Looks like you're about to be served with that subpoena," Mr. Bradshaw commented.

Yes, thought Alex with a sinking feeling, the subpoena and the end of any sense of safety he'd felt over the last two weeks.

The boys discussed their situation as soon as the officer had left. The trial date had been moved up to August the twenty-eighth, just over three weeks away. "It could happen anytime now," Alex said. He talked in a whisper, even though the bedroom door was shut and he could hear the adults making dinner in the kitchen. "You can't be alone anywhere from now on. Keep your pepper spray with you at all times. And going to Playland tomorrow is out." Despite everything else he was feeling, he was pleased to find a way to cancel that date.

"Oh yeah?"

"Yeah. It would be way too dangerous."

"Tough. I'm going. And you're coming with me."

"No, we're not, Tanner."

"Why not?"

"Because we'd be way too vulnerable. In Hap's mind he's got to get rid of us. He will know that there was a cop here today. He's going to follow us and as soon as he gets the opportunity — bang, we're gone."

"Bang?"

"Well, hopefully not 'bang', but you know what I mean."

"But you think we'll be safe in a crowd?"

"Safer. But not safe."

"Then we'll have to be in a crowd."

"Yeah, well, it's always crowded at Playland, but that's not what I meant."

"How about if Zoe and Caitlin come with us?"

Alex sighed. "Yeah, that would help, I guess. But we don't want to put their lives in danger."

"He doesn't want them. They won't be in danger."

"I suppose."

"Let's get them over here tonight and we'll tell them what's going on."

"Everything?"

Tanner glanced out the window. "Yeah. Everything. So that if something does happen, they'll at least know what it's all about."

Alex realized he'd just given in to Tanner. "I guess I'll have to start tomorrow then."

"Start what?"

"Leaving myself open, so he can abduct me."

"You don't have to do that, you know."

"Yeah, I do. It's our only chance. If he gets us both, we're dead."

Tanner nodded thoughtfully.

"And I guess Playland is as good a place to start as anywhere."

"But not until after we meet our birth mom."

Alex shook his head. "I can just see it. I'll get nabbed but you'll be so busy checking *her* out that that you'll forget all about me. I'll be killing myself sending you a picture and you won't even be trying to pick anything up."

Tanner opened his mouth to answer but stopped when he heard the phone ring. A moment later, Mr. Bradshaw was at their door, handing the portable phone to Tanner. Alex watched Tanner's face soften when he recognized the caller's voice. It must be Zoe, he thought. Only Zoe brought that goofy expression to his brother's face.

Smiling at whatever she was saying, Tanner glanced at Alex and then left the room with the portable phone. Alex heard the door to the den shut behind him. That was something else Tanner gained by having his vacation extended. More time with Zoe. Probably not a good thing, though, he thought. It'll make it that much harder to leave at the end of the summer. He would know. He'd left Cara behind last October. If he'd known then that it would end their relationship, he wondered, would he have done it?

Probably not.

.... twenty-one

For the second time in less than a week, Tanner lay awake most of the night. Possible scenarios of the next day's reunion with his birth mom ran through his mind like takes from a movie in progress. He'd been longing for this reunion ever since he'd met Alex and had discovered he was an adoptee, but he hadn't been foolish enough to think it would happen so quickly.

But it had.

In two short weeks he had initiated a search, contacted his birth mother and set up a reunion. In that same time period he'd also had a week of hockey camp, a week at the university with Dr. Montgomery, he'd practically been murdered by Alex's dad and he'd met Zoe, hot and wicked Zoe, who was coming onto him big time. He also knew his life was in grave danger until after the trial.

No wonder he was having trouble sleeping.

He listened to a plane thundering overhead as it made its final descent into the Vancouver International Airport. For a moment it sounded close enough to land on their roof, but then he heard it pass over the house. His thoughts returned to the day that lay ahead. Would he recognize his mother immediately? Would there be that instant connection between them that he'd read about in so many of the reunion stories on the Internet? What would they talk about?

What if he felt nothing – only ambivalence? Was that possible? Perhaps she was a fake. This could be a set-up; she could actually be some kind of sicko who'd read his postings and had decided to string him along. He'd never actually talked to her, only read her messages on the computer screen. Tanner shook his head and flipped over. No. She knew too much about the circumstances of their birth. She was for real — his mother. He was her flesh and blood — one of the twins she had given up for adoption over fifteen years ago. And besides, why would anyone want to pretend she was his mother if she wasn't?

Tanner mentally reviewed the list of questions he planned to ask her. Did he have any half brothers and sisters? How about grandparents, aunts, uncles, cousins? He'd save the most important questions for last, the questions about his biological father. Had she kept in touch with him? Did she ever tell him about the twins she had put up for adoption? Had *he* been wondering about *them* for fifteen years?

Tanner sighed and flipped onto his back. He could hear Alex's slow and steady breathing. Reluctantly, his thoughts turned to images of Alex getting abducted. He understood why Alex felt he had to do this, but didn't know how he could actually go through with it, knowing full well what Hap was capable of doing to him. "Torture" was not too strong a word to describe it. Alex was a lot braver than he was. Maybe living with an abusive father makes you tough, he thought. And besides, if Alex didn't make himself the martyr, then they both might be killed.

Damn! Thoughts of the abduction had messed up the good feelings he'd been having at the prospect of the reunion. And the anxiety of an abduction possibly happening at Playland tomorrow would really ruin a joyful first meeting.

Once again he wondered why Alex was so unsupportive of his search and almost fearful of this reunion with their mother. He knew it had something to do with the guilt he felt for running away last fall and for the scare that he had put his mother through. It seemed he felt honor-bound to protect her from any more trauma. But his mother was a grown woman; she could take care of herself. Alex needed to break away from her, live his own life. He was fifteen, practically an adult. He wouldn't always be there to protect her.

Maybe Alex was just using his mother's anxiety as an excuse. Perhaps he was really the paranoid one. But why? He had nothing to lose; his dad was a creep and he wouldn't be abandoning his mom — just solving the mystery of his roots. They had a right to do that.

So what was it then? What were Alex's insecurities that were making him so cautious? Tanner loved his mom and dad — this reunion had nothing to do with that. Surely Alex's mom would understand that too. What was it Alex had said the other night when they received her first e-mail? *She chose to give us up. She didn't want us.* Could he be pissed off at her? Someone he'd never even met?

Another plane roared overhead. The house vibrated slightly. How had he slept through all this noise in the past two weeks?

Tanner pulled a blanket over his shoulders. The house was finally cooling off. He thought again about the questions they'd had to answer for Dr. Montgomery this past week. It was clear to all of them that the different homes they'd grown up in had greatly influenced their personalities. At the end of one session, the doctor had asked them what they had learned from the tasks they'd completed. Tanner jokingly boasted that he was far more adventuresome, outgoing and happy-go-lucky than his brother, so those must be personality traits influenced by environment. Alex grudgingly agreed but claimed he was the more reflective, sensitive and compassionate one. That may be true, Tanner thought now, but he was also the more neurotic one.

The sound of birds chirping pulled Tanner out of his reverie. Dawn had finally arrived and he knew he had to get up and do something. It was impossible to lie still another second. He dressed quickly, slid his pepper spray into his pocket and crept out of the quiet house. It was a beautiful morning, so cool and fragrant. He took a deep breath. He knew it was dangerous to be out alone, but strenuous exercise was the only way for him to calm his jitters. He wheeled one of the bikes from the garage out through the side door, mounted it and began pedaling toward the dike. He rode hard and fast along the deserted path. It was too early for the usual crowd of joggers and walkers to be out and Hap wouldn't expect him to be up yet either, would he? He cleared his mind of the clutter that had kept him awake all night and concentrated solely on pedaling. It was the perfect summer morning — there was a cool breeze off the water but he could already feel the warm rays of the just risen sun on his skin. He pumped hard, pushing himself until his muscles burned and throbbed. Then he pumped some more.

Without warning, Alex's words were suddenly in his head. *Bang, we're gone.* He brought the bike to a screeching halt. He looked around at the isolated landscape. What the hell was he doing out here? He must be crazy!

He wheeled around and rode home as fast as he could.

....

Zoe and Caitlin arrived after breakfast and the four of them checked the bus schedule and selected a route that took them to Playland. The girls had come over the evening before and had listened carefully to the boys' plans.

"Cool," was Zoe's response to the news of the planned reunion, and Tanner was fascinated to see how excited she seemed by the element of danger. Caitlin, on the other hand, seemed intrigued by a reunion but once again tried to talk Alex out of placing himself in danger.

"There's no other way, Caitlin," he told her. "As long as Tanner does his part, I'll be fine."

Tanner wondered if Alex really believed that.

....

"How will you know it's her when you see her?" Zoe asked Tanner. They were on the bus, chugging toward Vancouver.

"She said she'd be under the old roller coaster and she told me what she'd be wearing. I'm assuming I'll just know her, anyway. That's how it happened in all the reunion stories I've read."

"Are you going to introduce Caitlin and me?"

"Sure. But give us a few minutes first, to, you know ..."

"Hug and kiss and cry?" Zoe smiled.

"Yeah. Something like that." He smiled back. He wasn't one to get choked up very often, but this might be one of those rare occasions.

They arrived at the amusement park and entered the gates. It was still morning, but smoke from barbecues grilling hamburgers wafted across the fairgrounds. Tanner swallowed hard as they passed a booth where sweet-smelling cotton candy was being rolled onto paper cones, and he hungrily eyed the soft pretzels being sold at another stand. He remembered his sister once saying that fairs were about food. It seemed that Playland was about food too, as well as noise, people and gypsy-like vendors hawking their wares.

There was still an hour to kill before the reunion. Tanner

and Alex leaned against a wall, waiting while the girls rode the Tilt-a-Whirl. They'd discovered another trait they shared — they both got sick on rides that spun you in circles.

Tanner felt rather than saw Alex jump, as if he'd received an electric shock. He glanced at him and saw how pale he looked.

"You okay?"

"Yeah. Sort of." He was studying a couple of young men who were approaching them. Tanner could feel how tense his brother was getting, but the men passed without even glancing at them.

"We're not going to get abducted in front of all these people, Alex."

"Maybe not. But I've still got the creeps. I guess I will until it happens."

Tanner didn't want to think about it. Alex had been a different person when they were out at the university last week. Happy. Enthusiastic. But the old Alex, the depressed and frightened one from the first week of his holiday, had taken hold again, only now twice as bad.

"Let's get some food," Tanner suggested when the girls rejoined them. They went to a concession stand, bought hot dogs and drinks, then sat at a picnic table to eat. Tanner watched the women that walked by them, hoping their mother might also be killing time while she waited to meet her long-lost sons. She'd said she'd be wearing denim shorts and a white T-shirt. But no one fit the picture he had of her in his head. In fact, some of the girls that wandered by them made even Zoe look tame. There were more shades of red, green, purple and blue hair than he'd ever seen, and gold and silver hoops of all sizes were dangling from each and every imaginable body part. Summer clothes — shorts and tank tops — were perfect for displaying body jewelry.

"You fit in perfectly with this crowd, Zoe," he commented.

"Thanks," she said. She put her hand on his head and ruffled his hair. "And we'll have you nicely bleached and spiked before long."

"Over my dead body."

Tanner felt Alex cringe again. "Sorry. It's just a saying."

"I know."

But Tanner could see that his brother was looking more and more tense. He glanced at his watch. "Only fifteen more minutes. You won't do anything stupid 'til after we've met her, right?"

Alex nodded. "I've come this far. I've got to meet her now."

"*Then* you'll get yourself killed." Caitlin narrowed her eyes and nodded. "She'll like that."

"You're sounding like a mother, Caitlin."

"Maybe I just know how a mother feels when she wants to protect someone she cares about."

Alex turned away. "Oh my God!" he exclaimed suddenly. They all turned to look. Alex's father was approaching their table.

"What are you doing here?" Alex demanded. "There's a restraining order on you. You're not allowed to be near us."

"Oh c'mon, Alex. I'm your father." He glanced at Tanner, and then back at Alex. "You *are* Alex, aren't you?"

"Yes, I am." He stood up, meeting the man face to face. "How did you find us here?"

"I followed you, of course. Any fool could do that. And I need to talk to you, Alex. Just for a few minutes." He raised his hands in the air. "Just talk. I promise."

Alex glanced at his watch. "We're meeting someone in just a minute. This isn't a good time."

"It will only take a minute, really. But I'd rather talk to you alone."

"You'll have to make an appointment to see him later." Tanner stood beside Alex, his arms crossed. "Alex told you, we're about to meet someone."

"Just talk to me now, Alex," his father pleaded, totally ignoring Tanner, "and I'll never bother you again. But there's a few things I need to get off my chest before I go home."

"You better go to the meeting place, Tanner," Alex said, not taking his eyes off his father. "I'll be there in a few minutes."

Tanner studied him, then shook his head. "Uh-uh. You can't be alone." He turned to Mr. Swanson. "Spit it out now. You've got two minutes."

Mr. Swanson shook his head. "This is a private matter, between a father and his son. C'mon, boy," he said to Tanner, "just give us a few minutes."

Tanner remembered pointing a knife at this man. He could feel the same hatred begin to stir in him again.

"I'll stay with Alex," Caitlin suggested. "At a distance," she said to Mr. Swanson. "Zoe, you go with Tanner and we'll meet you over there in a few minutes."

The four of them looked from one to the other and then they each nodded. Caitlin's suggestion would have to do. It was almost noon and it didn't seem they'd be able to get rid of Mr. Swanson any other way.

They tossed their wrappers into a garbage can and then Tanner and Zoe headed in the direction of the rickety-looking old roller coaster. Alex, his father and Caitlin began to walk in the opposite direction. Tanner turned and watched them go. He didn't like it. Not now, especially. But what could he do?

He looked up at the ancient structure of the roller coaster and watched as a train slowly inched up the first hill. Then he heard the screams of its passengers as it was released from the conveyer belt and sped down the tracks, propeled only by gravity.

He felt his stomach grip with excitement. Now this was a ride he'd enjoy going on. Maybe later.

He turned to Zoe. "Why don't you wait over there," he said, pointing to the entrance of the arcade, "and we'll either join you in a few minutes or you can come and find us here."

"Okay," she said. She grabbed him around the shoulders and hugged him. "Good luck."

"Thanks." He watched as she walked away, but just before she got swallowed up in the crowd she whirled around, winked and blew him a kiss. He smiled, blushed and then began looking around for a lady in a white T-shirt and denim shorts.

There were lots of denim shorts, and lots of white T-shirts, but no one who seemed to be looking for him.

A tap on his shoulder made him jump. He spun around.

"Tanner?"

"Yeah." He found himself standing face to face with a woman. "You're ..." He didn't know what to call her. "Mom" wouldn't do, not yet, but he hadn't thought to ask her name.

"I'm Kathy. Your ..." She hesitated.

"Birth mom." Tanner finished the sentence for her. She looked much younger than he'd expected. His eyes scanned her face, looking for pieces of himself. Her eyes were dark brown, like his, and so was her hair. She was about the same height as him, but other than that, there was no striking resemblance. He looked at her eyes again. She quickly looked away. Shy, he thought. But there was something about the eyes that wasn't quite right. What was it?

"Where's your brother?" she asked.

"He got ... held up."

"Oh." She looked disappointed.

"But he should be here any second." His gaze combed the area of the amusement park that Alex had disappeared into. "He looks just like me," he said lamely. She glanced at her watch and then peered in the same direction as Tanner.

"How are you?" she asked finally, but with no real interest in her voice.

"Fine," he answered, but felt as uncomfortable as she looked. This was not going the way he thought it would. He had so many questions to ask, but didn't know how to start. Damn Alex, anyway. He should be here. And why wasn't she acting more interested in him? She was still peering off into the distance, looking for Alex. He'd expected her to be more emotional, burst into tears or something. That's what had happened in all the reunion stories he'd read. He even expected to get emotional himself. But his mom, Kathy, didn't look one bit teary-eyed.

"Why don't we sit over there and wait?" Tanner suggested, motioning to a bench.

"Actually, why don't we head over that way," she said, indicating the direction Alex should be coming from, "and see if we can find him?" She looked at her watch again.

"Okay," agreed Tanner. He looked toward the arcade but didn't see Zoe in the crowd. He glanced back at his birth mom. This was insane. Instead of acting overjoyed to see him she seemed cool and distant. What was with her? Hadn't she come here to get to know him? What was it she'd said in her first e-mail message?

Not a day has gone by that you are not in my thoughts. She sure had a strange way of showing it.

The voice of Alex popped into his head. *Maybe she's an idiot,* he'd said the night Tanner had broached the subject of doing a search. Maybe he was right, Tanner thought glumly.

They walked past the concession stand where they'd purchased their hot dogs, but Tanner didn't see Alex, Caitlin or Mr. Swanson. He peered into the distance, but the fairgrounds were getting extremely crowded and they could have headed off in any number of directions. Suddenly he felt a pang of alarm. What if Alex had been abducted already? Mr. Swanson said any fool could have followed them there. But then, where was Caitlin?

He turned and headed back toward the roller coaster. "I'm going to see if he's there yet."

"No, Tanner," she said, grabbing his arm. She looked at her watch again. "There's someone meeting us at the gate, and I don't want to miss him."

"There is?" Their father? It had to be!

"But Alex won't be able to find us."

"We'll come back and get him."

Tanner nodded, took one last look around and then hurried after her. He had to fight through the crowd to keep up. What's the matter with this picture? he thought. This woman was clearly not interested in him, yet she had contacted him and initiated this reunion.

Who's the idiot here? "Kathy!" he called. He would tell her that he was going back to find Alex.

She was standing at the exit now, watching the traffic. She glanced at him as he joined her at the gate. "Did you say something?"

"Yeah," he said, looking directly into her eyes, trying to read what he saw there. But he saw nothing. Nothing but a blank stare. "I was just about to tell you …"

Suddenly it hit him. Her eyes. The non-identifying adoption papers had said his birth mother had blue-gray eyes. This woman's were dark brown.

There was a screech of tires as a car pulled out of the traffic and up onto the sidewalk. A man jumped out and rushed toward them.

Tanner turned to run, but a burly giant was behind him, pushing him toward the car. He screamed, but his voice blended in with the screams coming from the dozens of amusement-park rides. A sweet-smelling rag was pressed against his face. He struggled to free himself, but within seconds he felt weak all over, and the last thing he remembered seeing as he was pushed into the idling car were those dark brown eyes — smug and deeply satisfied.

twenty-two

Alex let his father lead them away from the crowd in the amusement park, but when Mr. Swanson began approaching an exit gate Alex stopped, took Caitlin's hand and refused to walk any further.

"Say what you have to say, Dad, because I need to get back to my brother."

"I told you, I want to talk to you in private."

"Fine." Alex turned to Caitlin. "Why don't you wait over there, by the petting zoo. I'll find out what he wants and then I'll come and get you."

She nodded and walked away, glancing over her shoulder a couple of times before she reached the fence that enclosed the farm animals.

"She's kinda pretty, Alex. Reminds me of your old girlfriend back home."

"What is it you wanted to get off your chest, Dad?"

"Well, Alex, you're coming home with me and I'm not taking no for an answer. We're a family, your mother, you and me, and we belong together. You've had your holiday, you've made your point, but it's time to go home." He began to walk toward the exit again.

"Is that it, Dad?" Alex was incredulous. "That's what you followed me here for? You actually broke a restraining order to tell me that? Again? I thought maybe you had something new to say." Alex felt his anger build. "Now you listen to me. I'm not going back to Tahsis and you can't make me. And neither is Mom. We don't need you. And I have some place to be right now — with my brother."

Alex turned and began to storm away but his father grabbed his arm and swung him back around. He began to drag him toward the exit.

"Let go of me!" Alex yanked his arm away.

Mr. Swanson raised his hand and smacked Alex across the head. "You'll come with me now!" he ordered.

Alex hardly flinched. He felt, rather than saw, a small crowd gather around them. "Go for it, Dad." His voice was calm as he watched his father's arm rise to strike him again. "C'mon. Do it again," he urged. He gestured with both hands, egging him on. "I can take it." He watched his father's arm drop as he too noticed the circle of strangers gathering around them. "That's one thing I can thank you for, Dad," he continued, his eyes narrowed in fury. "You've made me tough. But that's all you've ever done for me." He continued to glare at his father. "Tanner should have charged you with assault when he had the chance, but he's too considerate, something you wouldn't know anything about."

They stood facing each other, a standoff.

Alex ignored the onlookers. "You gave up the privilege of being in our family, Dad. Family members love each other."

"Alex …" His dad straightened, staring at his son as if seeing him for the first time.

"Yes?"

"You've never stood up to me before."

"Yes I have. I ran away."

"That was a cop-out."

"No it wasn't. It was my way of dealing with you." He studied his father, noticing that he was regarding Alex with something bordering on respect. "Would you have preferred it if I'd swung back at you, maybe even getting mad enough to kill you at some point?"

"I'm sorry, son." His voice was thick with emotion.

"You're what? Sorry? For smacking me just now? Or for years of smacking me around? What are you sorry about?"

Mr. Swanson pushed his hands deep into his pockets. "I don't know how to handle this stuff very well. It's just that ..." His eyes looked pleadingly into Alex's. "It's just that I love you, and your mom. I need you to come home."

Alex sighed. "You don't know what love is, Dad. Hell, you're not even my real dad. But if you have any feelings at all for me, you'll leave me alone. I have to go find Tanner. He needs me right now." He paused, surprised that it took so little to stop his father's attack. "You should get help, you know. There are ways of dealing with your problems."

He turned to walk away.

"Alex."

Alex stopped walking, but he didn't turn back.

"What kind of help?"

Alex swung around, stunned. His father still stood there, looking pathetic. "You'd get some?"

"If I did, would you come home?"

Alex felt the circle of strangers tighten around them, waiting for his answer. He felt like he was part of a circus sideshow. "Do ya mind?" he asked, glancing around at the strangers. "Show's over." The small crowd dispersed slowly, leaving them alone again.

"Would you?" Mr. Swanson repeated.

"Why can't you just do it for yourself?"

"I love you more than I love myself."

"I find that hard to believe. You're always mad at me."

Mr. Swanson hung his head. "It's like I have no control of the anger. It just boils over. But you're wrong, you know." He looked at Alex again. "I am your real dad. In every way that counts."

Alex shook his head. "I can't promise to come home. But I would like things to go back to the way they were, the way they were when I was a little kid. Before things changed. Before you changed."

He noticed Caitlin approaching them with a security guard. "Everything okay here?" the guard asked.

Alex looked at his dad. A slow moment passed.

Mr. Swanson nodded slightly. "Yeah, it is now."

"You're sure? This young lady said you were fighting."

"We were," Alex said. "But we're not now." He looked directly into his father's eyes. "Everything's going to be okay, but thanks for checking."

The security guard looked from one to the other before turning and walking away.

"Caitlin and I have to get over to the roller coaster, Dad." A picture of dark brown eyes had just popped into his head and he knew it was Tanner's way of telling him to get over there, the reunion was happening. "But let me know how it goes." He reached out for his father's hand. Mr. Swanson looked reluctant, but eventually offered his hand to his son. Alex shook it solemnly, then took Caitlin's hand again and they began jogging across the amusement park toward the famous Vancouver landmark.

They found Zoe under the roller coaster, but not Tanner or their birth mother.

"Where have you guys been?" she asked anxiously. "You've been gone more than half an hour."

"I needed to deal with my dad. Where's Tanner?"

"I don't know. I watched a woman approach him and then they walked away."

"Which way did they go?"

"Back in the direction you went in. I got the feeling they were looking for you."

"What did she look like?" Alex felt the first real rush of curiosity he'd experienced since Tanner had started the search.

Zoe shrugged. "Nothing special. Brown hair, medium build, a little young, maybe, for having kids your age."

"That would be why she gave them up." Caitlin looked at Zoe, her eyes narrowed. "Isn't that what you would do if you got pregnant?"

"What are you getting at?" Zoe challenged.

Alex sensed the tension between them, but this wasn't the time to hash it out. "C'mon, you guys, we've got to find them." He led the way back toward the picnic area where they'd had lunch. But they weren't there. Then they searched the amusement park.

"He said he'd meet you at the arcade or by the roller coaster. That's it?" Alex asked Zoe for the third time. The alarm he felt was beginning to build.

Zoe nodded, appearing a little anxious herself. "Should we separate and search out different parts of the park?"

"No! Safety in numbers, remember?" Alex found himself breathing hard. He glanced at his watch. It was one o'clock. Tanner had met with their birth mother a full hour ago. He wouldn't be wandering around Playland that long looking for him. They would have checked back here — at the roller coaster — at least a few times.

Alex slumped onto a bench. He studied a train whipping

around the tracks. He remembered the image of brown eyes that had appeared in his mind as he'd left his father. He closed his eyes, visualized the train and pushed. He waited, expecting to get a reply, but there was nothing. He thought of the trophy, their signal, and pushed a picture of that. He waited. Still nothing. Where the hell was he? Had Hap abducted him right in front of their birth mother? But even if he had been abducted, wouldn't he send him an image?

Something was terribly wrong.

He jumped up. "Something's happened to him."

The girls looked at one another.

"Try phoning your uncle," Caitlin suggested. "Maybe he's checked in at home."

It was worth a try. They went to a pay phone and Alex dialed the number.

"Uncle John," he said when his uncle answered, "has Tanner called you or anything?"

"No, but then we just got home. Isn't he with you?"

"No. We went our separate ways for awhile, and now he's late meeting me." Alex hoped he didn't sound as anxious as he felt. "He's probably having a good time and ..." Alex couldn't go on. He knew it was nothing like that and there was no point telling any more lies. "Actually, Uncle John, I'm getting worried. I'm afraid something's happened to him."

"Is Zoe with him?"

"No, Zoe and Caitlin are with me."

"Let me just check the answering machine, Alex," his uncle said. There was a moment's pause. "Nope, nothing from Tanner. Are you still at Playland?"

"Yes."

"I'll be there in about forty minutes."

"Uncle John?"

"Yes."

"Bring Mom with you. We'll meet you under the roller coaster." He shook his head at the irony.

There was a pause. Alex knew his uncle wanted to ask more, but restrained himself.

"We'll be there in forty minutes, Alex."

Alex hung up the phone and turned to the girls. "They're coming down here."

"What are you going to tell them?" Caitlin asked.

Alex shrugged. "I don't know. I guess I'm going to have to tell them everything." He sank onto the nearby picnic table and squeezed his eyes shut. Damn Tanner anyway, he thought. Now it was going to be up to him to tell them about the reunion. His eyes suddenly snapped open. But something had happened to Tanner. That's all that mattered right now. He turned to Caitlin. "We're going to have to tell them about Hap."

"They'll make us go to the police."

He nodded.

"We can't do that, Alex," she pleaded. "He said he'd kill me if we went to the police."

"I know. But things aren't working out. Tanner's missing, and he's not responding to me. Everything's all screwed up. I think he's been abducted instead of me."

"But he was with your birth mother."

"I know. I don't know what happened to her. It's weird. She'd recognize me because I look like him, so if she were around she'd talk to us. And Zoe could tell us if it was her. She must have got scared off or something."

Alex tried sending his brother another message. There was no response. "Damn. The deal was that when I was abducted, I'd send the location we were being held hostage to Tanner. I don't know why he's not sending me anything."

"Maybe he just hasn't arrived anywhere yet," Zoe suggested.

"But he'd send me something to let me know we'd connected." Something was really wrong. "I'm going to phone Russell right now. Tell him to get over here too."

He saw Caitlin wipe her forehead with a trembling hand. "I'm sorry, Cait. But now we've got to protect ourselves, and this is the only way to do it."

He went back to the pay phone and called the police station. The girls stood glued to his side.

"May I speak to Officer Russell, please? This is Alex Swanson."

He listened, then said to the girls, "We're in luck. He's there." Another minute went by. "Yeah, it's me. Something has happened to Tanner. He's gone missing."

There was a pause.

"I'm at Playland, with two friends. My mom and my uncle are on their way down here right now." He listened. "Yeah, I think it does have something to do with Hap." Alex paused again. "Okay."

He hung up the phone. "He wants us to go straight to the station."

Half an hour later, Alex's mom and uncle found the three of them in front of the roller coaster. Alex had an arm around each girl, and they each had an arm around him. An onlooker may have thought Alex looked like a lucky guy, but he was feeling anything but lucky at that moment.

twenty-three

"There was supposed to be two of them."

"I know. Don't blame me. Only one showed."

Tanner vaguely recognized the female voice. He tried to open his eyes to see who was speaking.

"Now what are we going to do? He'll kill us!"

His eyes wouldn't open. He tried to wiggle his fingers ... his toes ... anything. But he was paralyzed. Couldn't move, couldn't speak. But he could hear.

"He won't kill us." The woman didn't seem to be bothered by the man's violent outbursts. "We work for him."

"Don't be so stupid."

Tanner heard a match strike and then smelled cigarette smoke. "Where'd he get you from, anyway?" the male voice continued. "You don't look like his type. He usually finds good-looking, smart women."

There was no response. Suddenly Tanner remembered who the female voice belonged to. His birth mom! Or the woman who'd said she was his birth mom. But ... how could that be? What had she done?

"We've got to think of something." It was the male voice again.

"I can't figure out why we're keeping them alive."

"Beats me," replied the growly voice. "I'd get rid of them. But you don't ask *him* questions." Tanner could hear the cigarette being ground out. "This is the only one that has to stay tranquilized. The boss heard weird things about him. Some parapsychological mumbo-jumbo. I think he's full of it, but we do what he says. The girl just has to stay tied up."

The girl? Was he talking about Maureen?

A picture of a roller-coaster train popped into Tanner's head. Alex was trying to reach him. Yes! He'd send a picture, call for help. Somehow he'd been abducted instead of Alex, but he knew what to do. He visualized himself, lying death-like, but alive. He tried to push, but couldn't. He focused on the old standby — the trophy — and pushed again. But it was no use. There was no energy. It was paralyzed too. His mind was as incapable of pushing a picture as his mouth was of speaking. Panic gripped him.

"So, how are you going to keep the boy alive?"

"You really don't know the boss very well, do you? We're each chosen for our special abilities." He paused. "Mind you, I'm still trying to figure out what yours are. But it just so happens I was almost an anesthetist at one time," he continued, "until I ended up doing time. But I know how to set up an intravenous line. They keep people in comas alive, don't they?"

"What were you doing time for?"

"Murder."

"So why aren't you still in prison?"

"I did my time." Another match was struck, another cigarette was lit. "But there will be a punishment far worse than jail if we don't figure out how to get the other kid. I suppose there is a point in keeping this one alive, just until we've got the pair. He might come in handy, a decoy perhaps ..."

Tanner wanted to scream ... to attack ... to kill.

But he couldn't move.

twenty-four

Alex was hit by a blast of cool air as he pushed open the door to the police station. The last time he'd been here was in the middle of winter, but except for the switch from stuffy heated air to cool air conditioning, the steady hum of activity was exactly the same.

Officer Russell met them at the door. Alex quickly introduced him to his mother, his uncle and the girls.

"I've got a meeting room for us," the officer said, "and some of the investigators are waiting for us there."

The group was led down a corridor to the same room Alex had been taken to last winter when he'd come to report all he knew about Hap's criminal activity and how he felt certain that Tanner, or Tanner's body, would be found at Hap's home. Today there were two men and a woman already in the room, file folders opened in front of them, pages strewn all over the table. The meeting must have started without them.

Introductions were quickly made. The team members assembled in the room were from the serious crimes unit assigned to Hap's case.

"So, Alex," Officer Russell stated. "You said you were supposed to meet Tanner at Playland, near the roller coaster at noon, but when you arrived, he wasn't there."

"Right."

"Where had you been?"

Alex looked at his mother. She returned the look, her eyes concerned. All she and his uncle knew was that Tanner hadn't shown up at a designated meeting place. Alex had suggested they wait until they'd arrived at the police station before he told them everything. They had agreed, though reluctantly. Mr. Bradshaw hadn't wanted to leave the park without conducting his own search, but Alex and the girls had assured him it was pointless. Tanner was not there.

They had hardly spoken all the way to the police station, and even Zoe was uncharacteristically quiet. But the tension had been electric.

Now he knew he had to confess to everything.

"My dad followed us to Playland this morning."

"But there was a restraining order on him," his mother argued, her cheeks flushed.

Alex sighed. And this was the easiest part of the story, he thought. "C'mon, Mom. You know Dad. No legal document was going to stop him from trying, at least one more time, to get me to move back to Tahsis with him. I think we've come to an understanding now, though."

She tipped her head to the side, hoping to hear more, but Officer Russell pressed on. "Your dad followed you to Playland. And ...?"

"He insisted on talking to me, alone. So I went with Dad, and Tanner and Zoe went to the roller coaster. Tanner was meeting someone there."

"I kept an eye on Alex," Caitlin said. "From a distance."

"Who was Tanner meeting?" the officer asked.

Alex looked at his hands, then at Caitlin. She nodded, encouraging him to go on. The room grew still, waiting. Alex swallowed. He could hear his own heart beating in his chest.

"Our birth mother," he whispered. The room remained still for a split second longer and then there was an explosion of questions directed at Alex. He ignored them all but looked at his mom. She regarded him quietly, puzzled.

"I told him to tell your mom!" Mr. Bradshaw's angry voice rose above the rest of the confusion in the room, which gradually grew quiet again as they waited for Alex to continue.

He spoke directly to his mom. "I didn't want him to do it," he said in a barely audible voice, as if there was no one else in the room. "But he was obsessed. He said he had to find his roots."

"I understand a lot of adopted kids feel that way," she answered. "I can understand it. But ..." She didn't continue, only looked at her brother anxiously.

Alex stared at her. He had completely underestimated her reaction. Totally. He shook his head. He was such an idiot.

"Anyway," he said, "he made contact with her on the Internet, and they were meeting today."

Mr. Bradshaw pushed back his chair and stood up. "We have a problem." He addressed the team of police officers. "That couldn't have been his birth mother."

"Why not?" asked Officer Russell.

Mr. Bradshaw looked at Alex, and then at his sister. He turned to Officer Russell. "May I speak to you alone, sir," he asked, "in the hall?"

Officer Russell glanced at the investigators. They nodded. Then he followed Alex's uncle into the corridor. They were back a moment later.

"Alex needs a few minutes alone with his mom and uncle," Officer Russell said to the gathered group. "You girls can go wait in the lobby. And we," he said to the investigators, "need to meet in Room Three, immediately." Everyone understood from the tone in his voice that the situation was serious. The room cleared quickly.

Mr. Bradshaw pulled a chair over beside Alex, who had moved so he could sit next to his mom.

"Why couldn't that have been our birth mom, Uncle John? He'd been searching on the Internet. He had a lucky break."

His mom shook her head. "There's something you don't know."

"That's why I told your brother to talk to your mom before he began," Mr. Bradshaw interrupted. "She's got some important information. I thought he hadn't started."

"What is it, Mom?" Alex asked.

"It's just that ..." She shook her head and sighed.

"If I'd known Tanner thought he was meeting her today," Mr. Bradshaw continued, his anger causing his voice to quiver, "this would never have happened."

"What do you mean, *thought* he was meeting her today?"

"Alex, your birth mom is dead," Mrs. Swanson whispered.

"How can she be dead?" He stood up abruptly, knocking his chair over. "She arranged a meeting with Tanner!"

"It can't be her, Alex," his mom answered gently. She reached for his hand. "There's been a mistake."

"Or he's been set up." Mr. Bradshaw's face was grim.

Alex's mind went numb. He couldn't think about this.

There was a quick rap on the door before it burst open. "Can we talk to Alex now?"

"Yes," said Mr. Bradshaw. "Come on in."

The detectives filed back into the room. Officer Russell remained standing, leaning against the door. He let the investigators take over the questioning.

"Alex," began the woman investigator, "we're worried that

Hap has abducted Tanner. I imagine that you must have come to that conclusion too."

Alex just stared blankly at her.

"We think Hap must have penetrated Tanner's search and set him up," she continued. "But what we need to know is how Hap knew Tanner was searching for his birth mother."

"All I know is Tanner was leaving messages on the Internet at a bunch of adoption sites. I guess it's how you go about doing a search."

"Yeah, but ..." The investigator rubbed her temple. "I can see how Hap could disguise himself on the Web if he knew Tanner was doing a search, but your own mom didn't know he was doing one. Or your uncle. It was a well-kept secret."

The room grew quiet.

"Is Zoe his girlfriend?" asked one of the other detectives, finally.

"Sort of. She's a friend of Caitlin's, and we met Caitlin at the library when Tanner first started his search."

The first detective sat up. "Could you two have been followed to the library?"

"Could have, I guess." Alex thought back to that night. He remembered his good intentions of being on the lookout for suspicious behavior, but when he'd spotted Caitlin his good intentions vanished.

"Did Tanner find books?"

Alex nodded. "He just typed in 'Adoption' on the computer and a whole list of them came up."

He noticed the look that passed between two of the detectives.

"I guess you don't remember whether Tanner left that list on the screen or went back to the main menu."

Yeah right, Alex thought. As if he'd remember something like that. But he did remember exactly what happened after

Tanner found the information on the computer catalogue. Tanner had spotted him ogling Caitlin and had stood at the computer terminal watching him watch her. "I suppose he may have left it on the screen because that's when we first spotted Caitlin."

"And did Tanner take out books that night?"

"No, he put them back on a shelf, but not the shelf they belonged on. He didn't want anyone else to come along and take them out before we came back the following night."

"So someone could have watched where he put them and discovered the topic he was studying."

"Could have."

"But it seems a bit of a stretch to think that a person could have found Tanner's postings on the Web so quickly and then convinced Tanner that he or she was his mother."

"Yeah, and this woman ..." Alex paused. "This *person* knew all the details of our birth."

"Well, she didn't get that information from a library book." The first detective crossed her arms and sat back in her chair again, still studying Alex. "Keep thinking, Alex."

He tried to recreate the night at the library in his mind but all he could remember was the powerful attraction he'd felt for Caitlin.

"Oh no," he groaned. "I'm so stupid." Once again, Tanner's abduction was all his fault.

"What is it, Alex?" He felt his uncle's hand on his arm.

"We'd written up a newspaper ad, stating our birth date and everything! Even our e-mail address. We left it on the table. Tanner thought I'd taken it, and I thought he'd get it after he shelved the books. But it was gone when he returned to the table." He covered his face with his hands. "I can't believe it," he mumbled. "We gave them just the information they needed. Practically handed it to them."

"We don't know that, Alex." His uncle's hand was on his back, the heat of it practically burning a hole right through him. Alex sat up, shaking it off. He didn't deserve to be comforted. He knew better than to leave information like that lying around.

"You said Zoe was with Tanner when he met this person today?"

"Not with him, but watching from a distance. She saw the lady that showed up."

Another look passed between the investigators. The woman cleared her throat. "We need to talk to the girls. You stay here, Alex, and try to remember anything else that might help us. We'll take the girls to the other room." She got up and collected her things but then noticed Alex's grief-stricken face. "We're going to find your brother, Alex. And then we're going to send Hap to jail for the rest of his life."

Alex nodded but he knew they were just words. A thought was beginning to take shape in his mind, but he had to suppress it, he knew it was too big. He watched as the investigating team left the room. Officer Russell stayed behind for an additional moment.

"Don't you and Tanner have some ..." Officer Russell tilted his head, as if he was not quite sure how to express it, "some ... special way of communicating?"

"Yeah." Alex had been trying to push pictures to Tanner for the last two hours, without success, but he didn't tell the officer that.

"This would be a good time to try and contact him, then, wouldn't it?"

Alex could see he was having trouble making the suggestion. It meant he had to admit to himself that he believed their telepathy existed, and that was not easy for someone who generally relied on only tangible evidence to solve problems.

Alex shrugged. Once again, he had to push away the tiny, pesky thoughts that were coming together to form a horrendous whole in his mind. The thoughts were like minuscule metal shavings as they gravitated toward a magnet, becoming a whole instead of insignificant little pieces. He couldn't let his scattered thoughts become that whole. He knew it would be too huge, too ugly.

Officer Russell left the three of them alone, instructing them to call for him if they thought of anything important.

"We need to talk, Alex." His mom's voice was gentle but insistent.

Alex didn't want to talk. He didn't want to listen. He just wanted to concentrate on keeping the thought from forming in his head.

"There's a lot you haven't told me, isn't there," she continued. It wasn't an accusation, just a statement.

Alex turned to look at his mom. "There's stuff you haven't told me either," he said.

"Then why don't we tell each other all we know right now," she suggested.

"I think you know everything now," he answered dully.

"Okay, then, what do you want to know from me?"

Alex studied her. Did he dare ask about the birth mother — the dead birth mother — that Tanner thought he'd been meeting that afternoon?

She knew what he was thinking. "You want to know how we knew your birth mother was dead, right?"

Alex nodded.

"Then I'll tell you."

Alex watched his mom's face. She seemed to be trying to remember something.

"Let me tell him what I can," said Alex's uncle. His mom nodded. "As you know, Alex," he continued, "my wife, your

Aunt Theresa, was a nurse. Shortly before you were born, she was the head of nurse's training, the preceptor, and there was always a large crew of student nurses that she oversaw. There was one student, though, a girl named Gabrielle, who she took special interest in. Gabrielle was particularly bright and out-going and your aunt had high hopes for her. But one day she simply didn't show up for work and it was rumored that she was considering dropping out.

"Theresa was quite concerned, so she tried to contact her, but Gabrielle wouldn't take any calls. And she did withdraw from the program. Well, your aunt was a stubborn woman so she paid a visit to her home. That's when Gabrielle told her she was pregnant. As I recall, the girl's parents were fairly supportive, but were insisting on two things. Firstly, they wanted the name of the father and secondly, they wanted her to promise that the baby would be put up for adoption.

"Your aunt told me that Gabrielle was very unwilling to agree to either. I don't believe she ever did name the father. However, your aunt had a plan. She knew that my sister, your mom," he looked at Alex's mom and she nodded, "wanted to have a child but was unable to."

His mom continued the story. "Your dad was dead set against adoption for some reason. He was afraid that we'd end up with a child who was, in his words, 'inferior' somehow. But when Theresa called and said she knew of a lovely, smart girl who might be convinced to give her baby up for adoption, I managed to get your father to agree. Theresa talked Gabrielle into it, pointing out that she, Theresa, would be the baby's aunt, so we got a lawyer and set up the terms for a private adoption."

Alex's uncle took over again. "But what the girl didn't know was that she was carrying twins. Only one heartbeat had been detected and the girl didn't have any other tests that may have determined that there were two babies.

"Well, when you two were born, all hell broke out. Your dad wanted to break the adoption agreement because he said that he'd only consented to take one baby and he refused to take two."

Alex's mom twisted her ring around and around her finger. "And this is the worst part of the story, Alex," she said sadly. "I did something very selfish, that in a way I deeply regret but in a way I'm still very glad that I did. I agreed to take only one of the babies and allowed the other one to be put out for adoption by the Children's Aid Society."

"Why would you agree to that?" Alex blurted out.

"Because I so desperately wanted a baby. I thought that this might be my last chance. And I'd been told I was getting Gabrielle's child. I was counting on it and I couldn't bear the thought of not having one. And you know your father — there was no way of changing his mind."

"Why did our birth mom, Gabrielle, agree to it?"

John Bradshaw answered. "Gabrielle went into such a state of postpartum depression after you two were born that she was barely functional. Apparently she held each of you and then kissed you good-bye. She knew she was unable to raise you herself, but I guess the thought of giving up two babies was more than she could handle and she virtually shut down. Theresa was extremely concerned about her. She visited her every few days after you were born.

"Anyway, you went to your mom and dad, Tanner went to Edmonton, and then when your dad decided that you were never to know you were adopted, the rest of us had to put it out of our heads too, like it or not."

His mom was shaking her head. "I'm sorry, Alex. We were all so intimidated by him." She sighed. "But, looking back at it now, I'd probably do it the same way again. Any other way and I wouldn't have had you."

Alex wanted to tell his mom it was okay, but he couldn't find the words. His head felt fuzzy and his tongue thick.

"Having Tanner here this summer has been an uncomfortable reminder for me," she continued. "Every time I see you two together I think of what could have been and what I did to you. You were meant to be together. I should have let you both go. You were only separated because of my selfishness."

"Not yours, Pat, Frank's." There was a long, painful silence.

Finally Alex found his voice again. "You still haven't told me how you know she's dead."

"You're right," Mr. Bradshaw said. "And please keep in mind, Alex, that what happened to your birth mom was no one's fault. It was mostly a physiological thing that happens to some women after birth, but was especially intense for her because of her loss of both babies. As I told you, Theresa kept visiting Gabrielle long after your birth, and she was very worried about her because her depression was so deep and devastating. But eventually Gabrielle seemed to perk up. She started making plans again and we thought she was out of the woods. And then she shocked all of us by taking an overdose of the antidepressant medication she was on and died. It made no sense, although people who are planning suicide often seem to perk up right before they take their lives." He shook his head. "It was a terrible waste. She was a lovely girl."

So she killed herself, Alex thought numbly. His own mother. Her name was Gabrielle and she'd committed suicide. How would Tanner feel about this?

The thought fragments grew dangerously close together in his mind.

"You look overwhelmed, Alex," his uncle said. "I think your mom and I will go see if we can find some coffee or something, and give you a minute to collect your thoughts."

Alex nodded. He *was* overwhelmed.

His mom, his adoptive mom, the woman who'd agreed to separate him from his brother, gently rubbed his back then left the room with his uncle.

He shook his head and tried one last time to contact Tanner. He concentrated on the shape and form of the Lions Gate Bridge — knowing Tanner would understand the significance if he received it — and then pushed as hard as he could. Then he let his mind go blank, opening it as wide as possible and hoping to find the shape of a gold trophy there.

But nothing appeared. His mind stayed blank.

Why wasn't Tanner responding? He hadn't been able to master the knack of blocking Alex's pictures at UBC last week. Alex was much better at it than Tanner ...

Suddenly the little snippets of thoughts in his mind flew together like the metal shavings would in one last attempt to reach their magnet. The truth hit him with such impact, such force, that Alex was jolted back in his chair.

He's dead.

Tanner's dead.

It was the only plausible explanation.

twenty-five

"Alex," a voice whispered, "is that you?"

Tanner vaguely recognized the female voice. He tried to open his eyes to see who was speaking.

"Alex? It's me, Maureen. I know you're coming to. You've been twitching."

His eyes still wouldn't open. But he thought he was wiggling his toes.

"Your foot is moving," the voice whispered. "You can hear me, can't you?"

He wiggled his foot as hard as he could.

"Are you Alex or Tanner?"

Tanner thought about that. How could he answer with a foot wiggle?

"Sorry," the voice whispered. "Wiggle if you're Alex."

Tanner lay still.

"So, you're Tanner."

He wiggled furiously. He tried opening his eyes again. He could see little slits of light. He was able to see the outline of her body sitting beside him.

"Is Alex still out there, free?"

He nodded.

"Then he's our last chance. If they get him, we're all dead."

Tanner thought of Alex's plan to get himself abducted just as a picture of the Lions Gate Bridge appeared in his mind. Alex was worried! That was a good sign. Maybe he'd abort the plan. He tried to send the trophy image, but he still didn't have the strength. He sighed.

"They've got us in some kind of warehouse. We must be on a dock because I can hear water slapping and boat horns off in the distance."

Tanner grunted. It was the best he could do.

"It's just us in here, but there must be another room in this building. I tried screaming for help when they first brought me here and suddenly people came running fast." She paused, remembering. "I won't do that again. I think it was a few days before I came to."

Tanner found he could turn his head to look at her. It was dark in the warehouse — there were no windows — but some sunlight was filtering in through cracks in the wooden plank walls. She was leaning against the wall beside him, her hands behind her back, probably tied, and there was twine securing her ankles together. Her face was covered in dark blotches. That looked like dirt, but he wondered if they were bruises.

He heard footsteps approaching from a long way off.

"It's her," Maureen said. "I can tell by the way she walks." They listened as the woman grew closer. "Close your eyes, Tanner. Pretend you're still unconscious."

He closed them just as the slit of light from the doorway opened onto a blinding ball of fire, the setting sun visible directly through the doorway. He'd remember that. The door faced west. He heard her approach across a wooden floor.

"I brought your dinner."

"I haven't had lunch," Maureen answered.

"Yeah, well, Max says there's no point fattening you up before the slaughter."

"I bet he thought he was pretty funny."

"Yeah, he did. Open your mouth. I've got to feed you because he's at an emergency meeting with the boss so I can't untie you."

It was quiet for a few minutes. Tanner thought maybe he too could hear water slapping against boards.

"How long have you been working for Hap?" Maureen asked, finally.

"Long enough. Here, have some water."

"Yeah? Long enough to think you're indispensable?"

"What do you mean?"

"I used to work for Hap," Maureen said, "and look at me now."

"Yeah, but you ran for it."

"That's right. I ran for it when I realized what was going to happen when he'd finished with me."

"And what was that?"

"He'd kill me."

"The boys say you took off because you got all soft over these kids."

"Why would I have brought Alex in if I was soft for him? I knew what Hap did with boys."

Tanner waited for the woman's answer, but there wasn't one.

"That gun Max packs around. Does it make you feel safe?" Maureen asked.

"Well, yeah, duh."

"He's just going to turn it on you when he's done with us."

"Why would he do that?" she laughed, but Tanner detected a nervous edge to the question. He reminded himself to keep his eyes shut.

"He'll be finished with you," Maureen said simply. "He won't need you anymore."

"I work for Hap." She made it sound like an honor.

"Only as long as he needs you. And he won't need you much longer."

A silence filled the stark warehouse. Tanner sensed the woman was considering Maureen's theory, but was surprised she couldn't see the flaws in it. Did she really believe Hap killed off all his employees after he was done with them? Couldn't she see it wouldn't take long before he couldn't find anyone to employ?

Heavy footsteps could be heard approaching the warehouse. Tanner heard the door bang open and sensed the room grow brighter, even with his eyes shut.

"Kathy! Get over here."

"All right already." Tanner heard her footsteps moving away. The door closed, but Max's agitated voice could be heard clearly through the wall.

"Hap's decided how to nab the other boy."

"Yeah, and?"

"It don't make sense."

"Oh."

Tanner strained to hear as the man's voice grew softer. "Some of the guys think he's losin' his touch. They're starting to make tracks."

"Make tracks?"

"You're really not very bright, are you?" The voice was loud again. "Hap must really have been desperate when he hired you. They're jumpin' ship. Movin' on. Do I make myself clear now?"

She ignored the question. "Why?"

Tanner was amazed she didn't stand up for herself.

The voice grew lower again, and Tanner couldn't make out any more words. Finally, the heavy footsteps clomped away and the door reopened. Tanner snapped his eyes shut and had to force himself to keep them shut when he felt a finger poke him in the ribs.

"I know you're there," the woman called Kathy said.

Tanner opened his eyes.

"You're off the drugs."

"Why?" Maureen asked. Tanner still didn't have a voice, but he found his body parts were starting to move more easily.

"Boss's orders."

"Which boss?" Maureen asked.

"Both." She quickly tied Tanner's hands behind his back with twine she pulled out of her backpack. She propped him up beside Maureen and then secured his ankles together.

"Now I'm going to have to feed both of you," she whined. She held a sandwich out in front of Tanner. He took a bite but found chewing required too much effort. He shook his head when she offered him more.

"You'll be back to yourself in a few hours."

He stared at her, wondering how he could have failed to notice she had the wrong eye color when he first met her.

"So, you're a twin?"

Tanner nodded.

"Me too."

He felt his eyebrows arch involuntarily.

"But I don't have any psychic powers with my twin."

Tanner glanced at Maureen. She looked as surprised as he felt.

"Wish *I'd* been chosen to be in a twin study. That would have been cool." Tanner forced himself to act unsurprised by her knowledge of his activities. It could be a trick. She held a water bottle up to his lips and he drank thirstily. He cleared his throat and tried to speak, but only a grunt came out.

She laughed at him. "You'll get everything back. He says it just takes awhile."

"I have to pee," Maureen said.

"Oh Lord," she complained, but fetched a hospital bedpan from the far corner. Tanner looked away while Maureen used it. Then Kathy untied his hands long enough for him to use it too, saying that she wasn't coming back that night and she didn't want to deal with a mess in the morning. Tanner gritted his teeth at the indignity of it. This was too much. "Have a nice night, guys," the woman said when she'd finished. She threw her backpack over her shoulder and stomped across the room. "I'll see you in the morning." Tanner watched her go through the door and heard her pause on the other side, probably fastening some kind of lock on it, he thought, and then her footsteps disappeared into the night.

"Hap knows everything," Maureen said, answering Tanner's unspoken thoughts. She was quiet for a few minutes, and Tanner realized that he too could detect the sound of boat motors on the water not far from where they were.

"I wonder if she was trying to set you up with that twin talk, if that's part of Hap's plan, or if she's really so stupid that she'd give away valuable information."

Nobody could be that stupid, Tanner thought miserably. Hap now knew about the one talent they had that they could use against him. How had he found out? Dr. Montgomery only told a few of his assistants about their gift, and no one that Tanner knew would have told anyone else. Somehow Hap had managed to penetrate the twin study. Perhaps one of the research assistants worked for him. Nothing would surprise him now.

But what had the man said? *Some of the guys think he's losin' his touch. They're starting to make tracks.*

Why now? What had happened? Was it something to do

with the way he planned to abduct Alex? Something to do with their telepathy?

He closed his eyes, focused on the trophy and pushed. It may have gone. But, then again, it may not have. He'd have to be careful. Hap was planning to use this skill against them somehow and he didn't want to draw Alex into any danger.

twenty-six

Alex jumped involuntarily when he heard the door open. He watched as the investigators, his mom, uncle, Caitlin and Officer Russell filed back into the room.

"Zoe is with our sketch artist giving a description of the woman who met your brother this afternoon, Alex," said Officer Russell.

Alex nodded.

"And Caitlin just filled me in on the phone call you made at her house."

He nodded again. He wasn't going to try and justify what he'd done or hadn't done. It was too late for that.

"Can you tell us exactly what happened that day, and any other information that you've been withholding?" The officer's voice was unrelenting.

Alex watched while one of the detectives pressed the record button on a tape machine. He told them about being followed to the park and about the envelope being dropped in his lap.

"Did you recognize the man?" asked one of the detectives.

"No. He had sunglasses and a ball cap on so it was hard to

see his features. Anyway, the note said 'two o'clock' and there was a phone number."

"Did you keep the note?"

"No." Alex frowned. He couldn't remember what he'd done with it. "I may have left it at Caitlin's."

"So, then you met up with Caitlin?"

"Yeah, and I told her what had just happened. She said I could use the phone at her house."

"So that's what you did."

"Uh-huh."

"Now, Alex, I want you to tell us what was said on the phone, as exactly as you remember it."

"It was Maureen who picked up the other end. She told me not to testify. She said they'd kill me if I testified."

"Are you sure it was her?"

"Yes, I'm sure. But she sounded awful."

"Did she say anything else? Anything at all?"

"No." Alex continued to stare at his hands as he told the story. "I asked her where she was but then someone else was on the phone — a man — and he said that I should 'heed' Maureen's words. Heed was the word he used." He glanced at Caitlin, but she didn't make eye contact with him. "Then he said not to go to you, or Caitlin would die too."

"Did he use the word 'die'?"

"No, he said she would 'go'. But it was clear what he meant."

"So that's why you didn't tell us about it." Officer Russell's voice had softened.

Alex just nodded.

"Caitlin also told us that she had been followed the night she met you at the library and that she had been questioned."

Alex glanced at her again and nodded. Was that really just two weeks ago?

The detectives and Officer Russell collectively slumped back in their chairs and studied Alex. He went back to cleaning his fingernails.

Finally, one of the detectives spoke again. "Is there anything else that has happened over the last two weeks, Alex, anything at all unusual that you can tell us?"

Alex regarded them for a moment, not remembering anything. A numbness had enveloped him and he could barely think. The word "dead" kept repeating itself over and over in his head. He glanced at Caitlin and watched as she removed the sunglasses that were propped on top of her head, nervously smoothed her hair back, and then repositioned the sunglasses to act as a hairband.

"Sunglasses," he said. "Tanner said there were two men wearing sunglasses who were watching him play hockey."

"That's good, Alex," the detective encouraged. "Anything else?"

He shook his head.

"Well, then,'" she shut the tape recorder off, "we'd better spell things out for you."

Alex nodded.

"You know that the criminal activity Hap's involved in is widespread, a lot wider than we originally anticipated. His trial date is only three weeks away, and we don't have nearly as much evidence as we'd hoped to at this point. They have covered their tracks brilliantly."

Brilliantly? It almost sounded like they admired Hap's operation.

"Unfortunately, Alex, with Maureen and Tanner missing, you are now the key witness in this case. And, of course, your safety is our primary concern. We need to employ a witness-protection program for you immediately. And, of course, we need to find out where they're holding Tanner and Maureen."

Should he tell them they wouldn't find Tanner — not alive, anyway?

"It was supposed to be me that was abducted," he said to no one in particular. His voice was flat, emotionless. "I was going to let them kidnap me, and then I'd send Tanner a mental image and he'd bring help."

"Alex, you're not serious." It was the first thing his mom had said in the past half-hour.

"It was the only way, Mom."

"So," his uncle asked quietly, "has Tanner sent you a picture?"

Alex shook his head. He decided to let him make the connection himself.

"Well, you know," mused one of the detectives, "Hap's people are going to be pressed to get Alex. They know that without him we don't have a case."

Seven pairs of eyes turned to look at the speaking investigator.

"We can use that to our benefit."

Mrs. Swanson jumped to her feet. "If you're thinking of putting Alex in any kind of danger, you can forget it. I won't allow it!"

Alex looked at his mom, amazed. She'd been remarkably quiet all afternoon, but this outburst was more emotion than he'd seen from her in a long time.

John Bradshaw pulled his sister back into her seat. "Let's just hear what he has to say."

"It's okay, ma'am," the officer continued. "We're not going to let anything happen to Alex. We want him alive as much as you do, but I'm just thinking aloud here. Hap's people aren't stupid, they're going to know that we're protecting Alex. But there's always a weak spot in every operation and they'll be looking for it. We just have to show them what it is, or what we want them to think it is, and we'll be able to lure them out of hiding long enough to nab them."

"Something could go wrong." Mrs. Swanson was shaking her head. "You're not using Alex to lure anybody out."

The detective turned to Alex's mom. "Mrs. Swanson, I hate to say this, but if we don't get Hap convicted, your son won't ever be safe again."

She glared back at him.

"We just have to make sure we are in control of this operation."

In control of the operation. Those words were almost as meaningless, Alex realized, as the ones he'd spoken to Caitlin just a few days ago. *My abduction has to be on my terms,* he'd said. Words, just empty words.

The room was quiet, but Alex could sense the wheels turning in the minds of the detectives. Finally, the woman pushed her chair back and got up. "We need a break," she said. "I'm going to have some dinner brought in, but in the meantime we need to confirm that Tanner's parents have been notified, and I'm going to check and see what's happening with the witness protection division. We'll reconvene after dinner." She turned to Caitlin. "And I need to talk to your and Zoe's parents immediately, so you can come with me."

Alex watched as everyone but his mom and uncle traipsed out again. He got up and began to pace around the room. The numbness that had settled over him when he realized his brother was dead was beginning to dissipate and a slow burning anger was beginning to fill his entire being. Hap had killed his brother, Hap had Maureen held hostage, and Hap had ruined his life.

Hap could not go unpunished. Alex would do whatever the police asked him to.

....

Later that evening, Alex and his mom and uncle went home accompanied by two plainclothes officers who would be guarding the house around the clock. The phone was ringing when they walked through the door. As he picked it up he noticed that the answering machine was flashing wildly. There must have been more messages than it could cope with.

"Alex." It was Dr. Montgomery. "Are you okay?"

"Yeah, I guess."

"I saw the story on the news. They said that Tanner's gone missing again."

"Uh-huh."

"What happened?" The despair in the research doctor's voice almost matched his own.

"It's a long story." Alex wondered how he could shorten it and then realized how much he'd actually like to see the doctor. "Why don't you come over?"

"Could I?"

Alex shrugged. "Why not? I don't think anyone will be sleeping around here tonight."

"I'll be there in twenty minutes."

....

Dr. Montgomery actually arrived in less than twenty minutes, but the plainclothes officers wouldn't let him in the house until they'd done a security check on him. Finally, Alex found himself alone in the den with him.

"And then when I went to meet him," Alex said, finishing off his retelling of the events of the morning, "I couldn't find him anywhere."

The doctor nodded. He had listened to the whole story without commenting.

"That's when we realized that something had happened." Alex couldn't keep his voice from warbling. He was getting tired and the day's crises were taking their toll.

Dr. Montgomery nodded. "What happened when you pushed him a picture?" he asked.

"Nothing." Alex couldn't make eye contact with him.

Dr. Montgomery didn't respond.

Alex stared at the ceiling, and then tried to focus on a face in one of the framed pictures that stood on the bookcase. He knew if he focused hard enough, he could stem the flow of tears that he felt pressing at the back of his eyes. "He's dead," he whispered.

Dr. Montgomery didn't move, but asked, very gently, "How do you know?"

"Because he doesn't respond to my pictures."

"That doesn't mean he's dead."

Alex's eyes moved from the picture of the stranger he was staring at to the one beside it. It was a picture of Tanner and him, taken last winter at the airport before Tanner left to go back to Edmonton. They faced the camera with their arms around each other, and they were wearing matching caps and T-shirts. That had reveled in their newfound sameness then, and Alex only knew which one was Tanner because there were still bruises visible on his face. He couldn't hold back the tears any longer. They poured down his face and his body was wracked by sobs. "He'd respond if he wasn't dead. There's no other explanation."

Dr. Montgomery waited while Alex let loose the outpouring of grief that he'd been holding back since early afternoon. "There may be another explanation, Alex," the doctor said, finally.

"And what's that?"

"I'm not sure, but I don't think you should draw those conclusions so quickly. You wouldn't want him to give up on you so easily."

Alex stared at the doctor, noticing how pale he'd become. Beads of sweat dotted his forehead. He thought Tanner was dead too, Alex realized, and was just trying to cheer him up.

Alex sat up.

"What is it?" the doctor asked.

"I think I saw the trophy, but it was really faint." He sighed and rubbed his eyes with the palms of his hands. "Maybe I'm just imagining it. Wishful thinking or something."

"Send him something! Let him know you got it."

Alex swallowed hard. He closed his eyes and pushed a picture of the trophy back. He waited. Nothing happened. "I must have been imagining it."

"Perhaps he's just very far away."

"I could send pictures to him in Edmonton."

"Well, farther than that, perhaps."

"Maybe."

....

Alex slept in the den that night. His room felt too empty without Tanner. As he lay on the couch he could hear his mom, uncle, Officer Russell and the investigators talking in the kitchen. He remembered the night last winter when he'd first heard Tanner's voice in his head, pleading for help. He opened his mind as wide as he could, but there were no voices and no pictures tonight. Finally, he fell into an exhausted sleep.

twenty-seven

"I've got pepper spray in my pocket."

"You do?"

Tanner couldn't see Maureen in the dark, but he could tell by her tone that she was excited.

"And you've got your voice back."

"Yeah. Finally." His throat was dry and scratchy but he could talk.

"That's perfect, Tanner. It might be just what we need to save ourselves."

"Yeah, but our hands are tied, literally."

"Only when Kathy's alone. When Max is here he unties my hands and lets me feed myself. And," she added bitterly, "do my own bedpan thing."

"Pepper spray won't overpower a gun."

"I know, but we have to wait for just the right moment. Max doesn't always carry his gun. With his big gut," she scoffed, "he probably finds it too uncomfortable. I was trying to convince Kathy to steal it or something. I don't know if it worked, though."

"She's a strange one."

"You haven't figured it out? She's a junkie. I wasn't kidding when I told her Hap would get rid of her. His house rule is you don't use drugs while you're on an operation for him. But she's ignored the rule and she'll pay for it."

"That's why she seems so dumb?"

"Yeah, well, she's probably stupid too. Stupidity and drugs don't mix."

"They don't? Seems to me you've got to be stupid to do drugs."

"Yeah," she agreed. "You're right. And it's a bad combination."

"So anyway, how will I know when I should use the pepper spray?"

"I'll let you know. And then we'll have to untie our feet, fast, and run like hell."

"Maybe we could get her to untie our feet first. Ask her to let us walk around the room a bit or something."

"It's worth a try. The important thing is, get as close to their faces as possible with that spray. And don't inhale it yourself."

Tanner nodded in the dark, then sat quietly for a few minutes, thinking about their escape. He felt Maureen shudder. "Are you okay?"

"Yeah, but it gets really cold in here at night. It's so damp."

Tanner thought about all the nights he'd practically suffocated from the heat in Alex's bedroom, and realized that Maureen had probably been down here shivering all that time. "Sit closer to me," he suggested, "and our body heat will help us keep each other warm."

"Thanks." He felt her wiggle her way closer to him and realized that she was shivering hard.

"Are you sure you're okay?" he asked.

"I don't know," she admitted. "I've been feeling really

crappy the last few days. Lack of food and stuff is probably getting to me."

The "and stuff" part was keeping clean, he realized as she huddled against him. He knew he wouldn't be smelling too good right about then either. But that was the least of his worries. As he leaned against her, trying to warm as much of her body with his own as he could, he heard her sigh and felt her body get heavier as she dozed off. With any luck, by tomorrow night they'd be out of here and back to safety. He envisioned the trophy one last time and pushed. He thought it went, but suspected it was too late. Alex would probably be sleeping.

....

It was still dark when Tanner tried sending another picture, but he knew it was getting close to morning by the sounds of the gulls outside. He tried to visualize Vancouver's waterfront but found his recollection was too vague, so he tried to think of something more specific. He conjured up a cruise ship, figuring there was always one moored in the city at this time of year. He pushed. Nothing came back.

Kathy came in alone later, and they had to put up with her feeding them again. As she held a dry sandwich up to his face, the kind you get from a vending machine, Tanner could see the needle marks snaking up her arm. Maureen was right. She was an addict. Maybe that was a good thing for them, he thought. If her judgment was impaired it just might give them the split-second advantage they'd need at some point …

"I thought about what you said about the gun," she said to Maureen.

"Yeah?" Maureen had her eyes closed and was leaning against the wall.

"I think I figured something out," she laughed.

"What's that?" Maureen's eyes opened into narrow slits.

"I'm not telling," she giggled again. "But give me a moment alone with it and I won't need to worry if he turns it on me."

Tanner was careful not to look at Maureen. He acted like it meant nothing to him that Kathy planned to tinker with the gun. He ate the sandwich she offered him, and as soon as she'd left the room he tried pushing a picture of a freighter to his brother. This time he was successful! A trophy came back immediately! Swallowing his excitement, he pushed the cruise ship picture again. A cruise ship picture came back. Now he had Alex's attention. What could he send him? He really didn't know where he was!

Tanner heard Max's heavy footsteps coming toward the warehouse a few minutes later, but they bypassed the room he and Maureen were in and carried on for a few paces. Tanner glanced at Maureen.

"Remember I said there was an adjoining room? It might be an office or something."

Tanner nodded. That must be where Kathy had disappeared to as well.

The low murmur of voices carried through the walls, but Tanner couldn't make out any words. Before long, the heavy footsteps could be heard approaching again. This time the door banged open and Max sauntered toward his hostages.

"How's it hanging, Tanner?"

Tanner refused to look at him or respond to the question.

"You can't fool me, boy. I know the drug has worn off. You're perfectly capable of talking now."

Tanner felt the man's stare. Then he saw him walk across the room and fetch a rickety, straight-backed chair that had been abandoned in a far corner. He carried it over to where they sat, twirled it around so it faced the other way and then sat down, straddling it, and studied Tanner. Tanner finally glanced at him and noticed, just as Maureen had said, that he didn't appear to be carrying his gun.

"So," he said in his growly voice, "there's been a new development."

Tanner made eye contact with him for the first time.

The man lowered his voice conspiratorially. "Most of us feel Hap has lost his grip on reality."

Tanner continued to stare.

"You see, Hap believes that you have some kind of telepathy with your brother. He thinks that if we let you know where you are, you will send some vibes to your brother and he'll head straight over here and rescue you."

The man waited for a response, but got nothing.

"Of course, he will bring the police and they'll try to bust us."

"And you believe Tanner can do that?" Maureen asked.

"Of course not!" he said. His derisive laugh became a hacking cough. He pulled a cigarette out of the package he kept in his shirt pocket.

"Can I have one of those?" Maureen asked.

"Yeah right," the man said, and turned back to Tanner, ignoring her. He lit the cigarette, inhaled deeply and blew out a long stream of smoke. "He thinks that if you knew you were here in this cabin on Grouse Mountain, you'd send him a message to take the gondola up here and rescue you. Oops," he added, "I shouldn't be givin' away all the boss's secrets, should I? You might telepath 'em to your brother." He laughed heartily again. "What a joke!"

Grouse Mountain? Tanner thought. He pictured the bright red gondola that traveled up and down the mountain that towered over the north side of the city. Did this Max guy actually think that he'd believe that's where he was? He decided to go along with the story. "How did I get up here?" he asked. "Did you bring me up the gondola?"

"Hell no!" Max laughed again, and then broke into the

hacking cough once more. "There's more than one way to scale this mountain, and I'm not talking about the Grouse Grind, either," he said, referring to the hiking trail that wound its way up the mountain's face.

Tanner was really confused. What was this man trying to do? Surely he realized that Tanner would sense it was not logistically possible to have them held hostage up there. So why was he telling them this?

Tanner glanced around. There were no windows in the warehouse, he remembered, and, aside from the blinding sunlight, you couldn't see anything from this side of the room when the door was opened that could help you determine where you were. It was only through hearing the water and the ship's horns in the distance, and feeling the dampness, that Maureen had figured it out. Max might not realize they could hear anything. The sounds certainly weren't obvious. It was just the acute stillness in the room that allowed them to hear anything at all, and it would be colder up the mountain, too. Maureen had also been unconscious when she'd been brought here, so he supposed Max might believe he was convincing her too.

Max was right, Tanner thought. Hap was losing his grip. This was a pretty lame story.

"Anyway," Max continued, "none of us buy this crap about you sending your twin messages, so the guys are defecting fast and furious. Everyone thinks Hap's days as boss are numbered. I'm not quite sure what to do myself. Once I get paid for this job I guess I'll split too."

A picture of a wharf, with boats tied up, appeared in Tanner's mind. Alex was trying to get some more information, but Tanner ignored it for the moment.

"There's not much point keeping you two alive much longer," he added. "Things just aren't going the way they were planned." He stood up, lifted the chair off the floor and heaved it across the room. They all watched as it hit the floor and flew into pieces. Then he stomped out and they heard him return to the adjoining room. Tanner thought he could hear a telephone ring through the walls.

"Alex is trying to figure out where we are," he whispered to Maureen. "What should I send him?"

She looked at him, startled. He could see that she looked feverish today. Her eyes were glassy and she was still trembling despite the fact that it had warmed up in the building.

"Show him the Lions Gate Bridge. I'm sure we're in the harbor."

"He might misinterpret that. We've used it before."

"Then show him the Second Narrows Bridge. Send him both. We must be somewhere down on the waterfront between them. That's where most of the boat traffic is, and it's also where most of the drug trafficking goes on."

"What does the Second Narrows Bridge look like?"

"It's orange, and it's not suspended from cables like the Lions Gate Bridge."

"Oh yeah. I remember it now."

Tanner took her suggestion. He sent first one bridge, and then the other. He hoped Alex would recognize the Second Narrows Bridge. He kept sending them, one after the other.

"Send him a picture of Grouse Mountain too," she whispered. "And tell him to send the police there. There must be some reason he wants your brother to go to that spot."

"I can't tell him anything. I can only send pictures."

"Then show him the gondola and a picture of himself being overpowered by some thugs."

It might work, Tanner thought. Like a picture story. He did what she suggested, alternating pictures of the gondola going up the mountain with pictures of a boy being forcibly grabbed by a larger person.

Alex sent them back, showing he'd received them, but what Tanner didn't know was whether his brother had understood the messages or not. The morning crept by.

Finally, the door banged open and Kathy and Max were back with more food. Tanner felt his heart pounding in his chest. Was this going to be their chance to escape?

But Max did have his gun this time, and he waited at the door while Kathy came over and untied their hands. Tanner groaned when he drew his arms around to the front of his body. They were stiff and very painful. Maureen, who'd been untied first, was gently massaging her hands, trying to get the circulation moving again.

"How about undoing our feet and letting us walk off the stiffness a bit?" Maureen asked.

Kathy glanced at Max, looking for permission. He stared at Maureen for a moment, then nodded and shut the door. He leaned against it, watching while Kathy undid the knots.

He was so stiff that it took Tanner a moment to stand. He leaned over Maureen and helped pull her up. She was visibly shaking and could barely straighten her back. Their eyes met and she nodded ever so slightly. His heart began to beat even harder in his chest. He took her arm and supported her as they slowly walked around the room.

Max lit a cigarette as he watched them struggle. "You know," he said to Kathy. "I'm tempted to kill these two right now and move outta here. The boss is getting too weird. I've got a bad feeling ..."

The ringing of a phone could be heard through the wall again. Tanner saw Kathy glance sharply at Max.

"Damn," he said. "I've got to get that." Max took a step toward the door, then turned. "Get back to the wall," he said, pointing the gun in their direction "Tie them up," he ordered.

They headed slowly back to their wall. Max watched them

for a moment, but grew impatient as the phone continued to jangle through the wall.

"Holler if you need me," he said, then laughed. "But they don't look capable of overpowering a flea."

Tanner helped Maureen back across the room. As they approached the wall, Maureen said, "Could I pee before you tie me back up?"

Tanner slid his hand in his pocket as Kathy turned to answer Maureen.

"No," she said. "Get back over here."

Tanner felt the lid of the pepper spray twist between his fingers and he clicked the top twice. His palms were sweaty and he hoped he wouldn't drop it. Then, as he reached the wall, he snatched it out of his pocket and held it directly in Kathy's face. Her eyes opened wide in surprise. She reached up and grabbed his wrist.

"Run," he said to Maureen. Then, taking a deep breath, he squeezed the trigger.

Kathy released her grip on Tanner as the spray hit her eyes and nose. She covered her face with both hands and began to scream.

Maureen had almost reached the door, but as Tanner turned to join her, Max was there, his gun cocked and pointed at her head.

"Drop it, Tanner," he said. Beads of sweat were visible on his forehead.

"Spray him, Tanner," ordered Maureen. "Free yourself!"

Tanner knew that if he sprayed Max, Maureen would be hit with it too, if Max hadn't already shot her.

"I said drop it, Tanner, now." Max's voice could barely be heard over Kathy's screams, which were growing louder and more desperate. Someone was bound to hear her.

"Shut up!" Max screamed at her. Then he turned to Tanner. "This is your last chance," he said. "Drop it or I shoot her."

Tanner lunged toward Max and Maureen. He saw Max pull the trigger and release it.

There was a quiet click, but nothing happened.

He pulled it again. Click. Nothing. He let go of Maureen to open the ammunition chamber. "What the hell!"

"Run!" hollered Tanner. He pointed the pepper spray at Max as soon as she'd moved away but it was too late. As soon as Max realized someone had emptied the bullets out of the gun, he turned his back. The pepper spray missed its target and hit the back of his neck.

Still holding the small canister, Tanner grabbed Maureen's arm and began hauling her toward the street. He turned and saw Max lumber into his office and knew it would be only seconds before he'd reloaded the gun.

"Quick!" he said, but he knew Maureen was sick and stiff from being tied up. It was impossible for her to hurry.

Tanner's desperation grew as they struggled toward the road. The warehouse they'd been held hostage in was at the end of a long row of warehouses that jutted out into the harbor. It was so far to go. There was no way they could get away.

Suddenly, Tanner saw a head appear from a hole where a plank was missing in the walkway. A couple more planks suddenly lifted up and a hand emerged.

"Down here," said a voice. "Quick!"

Tanner pushed Maureen down into the hole in front of him. He saw hands grab her around the waist. As soon as she was down, he slipped into the hole himself. He felt hands reaching above him, replacing the missing planks, and then he peered into the shadows.

.... twenty-eight

Alex opened his eyes and wondered why he'd been dreaming about cruise ships and freighters. Then he sat up, his heart pounding in his chest. Those weren't dreams — those were images sent to him by Tanner! Dr. Montgomery was right; Tanner wasn't dead! He concentrated on the image of the freighter he'd just received and sent it back. He waited. The cruise ship came back to him again. He sent it right back. What was this all about? Why pictures of boats? Did they have Tanner held hostage on the water somewhere, on a ship? Perhaps in one of the boats that the drugs were smuggled on!

Alex picked up the phone while he waited for another image and dialed Dr. Montgomery's home phone number.

"He's alive!" he said as soon as the doctor picked up the phone.

Alex heard the huge sigh of relief. "Thank God. Oh, Alex, you don't know how relieved I am."

"Yes, I do. Believe me."

"Actually, Alex, you don't."

What was the man talking about? "Why don't I?"

"There's something I have to tell you. Can I come over again?"

"Yeah, sure."

"He's sent you pictures, right? That's how you know he's alive?"

"Uh-huh."

"Well, don't tell the police yet."

"Why not?"

"I'll tell you when I get there."

"Okay, but come right now. I don't know what's going on around here, I'm not even out of bed yet, but come anyway. Hurry."

Alex went into the kitchen and found his mom and uncle sitting there, drinking coffee. They were still wearing the clothes they'd had on the day before and there were dark smudges under their eyes. "Didn't you guys go to bed last night?"

His mom looked up as she shook her head. "We were responsible for Tanner," she said simply.

He studied their weary faces. Should he tell them he knew Tanner was alive? No. They had never believed — like he had — that Tanner was dead.

He poured himself a bowl of cereal and looked out the window. "Where are the cops?"

"One is at the front door, one's at the back. It's two different guys today. You should go introduce yourself when you've finished your breakfast," his uncle suggested.

Alex nodded. "Dr. Montgomery is coming back this morning."

"He is? How come?"

"He just wants to, I guess."

"Tanner's parents will be here this afternoon," his mom said.

"Really?" He'd have to find Tanner before they got there. He couldn't face them any other way.

Alex went to the back door and opened it. The officer smiled. "You must be Alex."

Alex nodded.

"We'll keep you safe. You have nothing to worry about."

"Nothing?"

He smiled again. "You know what I mean."

"Thanks."

Alex went to the front door and had much the same conversation with the police officer stationed there. Then he returned to the den. He thought about the pictures he'd received. They were about boats and the water. He needed something more concrete to give the police. He thought of a wharf with boats tied up. He pushed and waited. Nothing came back. What was Tanner doing now?

Dr. Montgomery arrived a few minutes later and joined Alex in the den. Alex noticed that he looked as weary as his mom and uncle did, but even more distraught somehow. He paced about the room while Alex told him about the pictures.

"Alex, there's something you don't know," Dr. Montgomery said.

"What's that?"

"These pictures may be ... contaminated somehow."

"What are you talking about? How could these pictures be contaminated?"

"Alex, sit down. There's something I need to tell you."

Alex sat in the chair by the computer. "What?"

The doctor lowered himself slowly onto the couch. "Remember Vince, my assistant researcher at the university?"

"The guy with the diamond stud in his nose?"

"That's him. I went to work early one morning and found him on my computer. He said his was down, but I noticed how quickly he changed the screen he was working on when I came into the room."

A sense of dread washed over Alex.

"I told him my computer was off limits, but two days ago I found him at the fax machine."

"What are you telling me?"

"He was faxing my notes. Information about you and Tanner."

Alex stared at the doctor. "To who?"

"I didn't know then. I told him he was dismissed and he threatened me. Said he had friends who would 'take care of me' if I fired him. Of course I fired him anyway. Then yesterday, when I heard about Tanner, I tried to phone him."

"And?"

"He's ..." The doctor pulled off his glasses and wiped them on his handkerchief. Alex noticed his hands were shaking. "It seems he's disappeared. His phone has been disconnected and the address I had for him doesn't exist."

Alex flicked on the power switch for the computer. "But even if Hap knows about our telepathy, how do you think he could contaminate our pictures?"

"I don't really know. But I'm sure he has something planned."

The Lions Gate Bridge appeared in Alex's head. He sat up.

"What is it?"

"The Lions Gate Bridge." He put his hand to his temple. "Whoa. Now there's another bridge. I think it's the one just up the harbor from the Lions Gate."

"That would be the Second Narrows."

"Damn! There's the Lions Gate again! And now the Second Narrows! What's he trying to tell me?"

"Well ..." The doctor seemed to perk up. "He was sending you various ships before, and now these two bridges. Maybe he's somewhere on the water between the two bridges. On a boat, no doubt."

"Oh my God!"

"What now?" The doctor studied Alex, alarmed.

"Now I'm getting that gondola thing that goes up and down that mountain in North Vancouver."

"Grouse Mountain?"

"Yeah. And now there's two men beating him up — or maybe it's me — and carrying him away."

"Oh my God!"

"And now there's the bridges again, first one, then the other. What's he telling me?"

"Well, let's think. We know Hap's trying to influence his messages. I don't know. Send them back. Let him know you got them."

Alex sent them back and waited, but nothing else came.

"We've got to tell the police," Alex insisted. "And have them dispatch one unit to Grouse Mountain and another one to the harbor!"

There was a knock on the door before the doctor could respond.

"Yes?"

The police officer from the front door stepped into the den. "Alex, we feel it would be best if your friend left now."

"Why?"

"You don't need to know that. It's our job to keep you safe and we feel that this would be in your best interest."

"Well, I think you're wrong. I need him right now."

"Alex, I don't want to have to throw my weight around, but I've been given permission to do whatever it takes to keep you safe, and I believe that it's time for your friend to leave."

"Give me ten more minutes with the boy," Dr. Montgomery pleaded. "And then I'll leave without a fuss."

"I don't think so, sir."

"Well, I *do* think so," the doctor said.

The officer stepped into the room and took the doctor's arm. He pulled him off the couch and dragged him toward Alex, who'd stood up and was trying to block their progress.

"Step aside, Alex," said the officer. "I don't want you to get hurt."

"Let him go," Alex said. "He'll leave. Just let him go."

The officer studied Alex for a moment and then released his grip on the doctor's arm. The doctor rotated his shoulders, straightened his jacket and began to leave the room. But as he passed Alex he leaned down and whispered in his ear. "You can't trust anyone — not even the cops!"

The officer shoved the doctor toward the door.

"Just look what happened with my assistant!" the doctor added, before being pushed right out of the room.

"And leave quietly," the officer admonished. "The kid's mom and uncle are trying to sleep."

Alex slumped into the chair. Could the doctor be right? He swallowed hard, not wanting to accept the possibility. But if Hap had managed to infiltrate Dr. Montgomery's work, what kept him from having an informer on the inside of the police department? Hap did seem to know things as soon as the cops did.

Alex stared blankly at the flickering screen saver on the computer monitor. What should he do now? He pushed a picture of a cruise ship to Tanner. Nothing came back. He tried the Grouse Mountain gondola again. Still no reply. He put his hand on the mouse and pointed the cursor to the Internet icon and waited for the screen to appear. He checked for e-mail. There was one new message. Alex read it and felt the overwhelming numbness from the previous day return. Just like the very first letter he'd received from Hap, this one was short and to the point.

You are dead meat.

He shut off the computer without exiting the program and

left the den. Sure enough, his uncle was stretched out on the living room couch, sleeping; his mother was nowhere to be seen. He sat down at the kitchen table and lay his head on his hands. He closed his eyes and willed his brother to contact him.

There it was — a new picture! But what was it? It seemed to be the inside of some kind of wooden cavern. Then another picture, but it too was unclear. There was a wood beam floor, and he could see water below it. Then another picture. Sunlight filtering through cracks in a plank ceiling.

It was too weird. He didn't get it. He didn't know what kind of a message Tanner was sending. He sent the gondola picture back but the reply was quick and straightforward. He saw a warehouse with no distinguishing features.

So, Alex thought, he was near the water, possibly in a warehouse, and he could see water below him through the floorboards. That was a strange warehouse. Alex sent it back to confirm he'd seen it.

A new picture arrived, an image of Canada Place, complete with sails. Canada Place was the convention center located on the waterfront in Vancouver's harbor. Lions Gate Bridge was in the background, so Tanner was somewhere to the east of it, in a warehouse, on wooden beams that lay over the water.

He reached for the phone. He was going to phone Officer Russell, but stopped before he pressed the last button. *Don't trust anyone, even the cops,* Dr. Montgomery had said. Well, he knew he could trust Officer Russell, but even he might inadvertently talk to the wrong person. He hung up the phone and then picked it up and dialed another number.

"Hello?"

"Caitlin. It's Alex."

"Hi, Alex. Any word on Tanner?"

"Come over here now," he whispered into the phone. "And bring Zoe."

"Why?"

"I'll tell you why when you get here."

"I can't."

"Why not?"

"I'm not allowed out."

"Then sneak out, but get over here right now. Before it's too late."

"I can't, Alex."

"It's a matter of life and death, Caitlin. Come now." He hung up the phone before she could argue anymore.

He went to his bedroom and found the business card Officer Russell had given him way back when they'd first met at the coffee shop. Then he went to the kitchen and watched for the girls to arrive. They just *had* to come. There was no one else who could do this for him.

A few minutes later he saw the two girls hurrying up the sidewalk. He jumped up and opened the front door. The officer who had kicked the doctor out was standing there.

"What are you girls doing here?" he demanded.

"We just came to keep Alex company."

"He's not allowed any visitors today," the officer said. "Run along home now."

"Who says?" Alex asked.

"I says," the officer said.

"And why is that?" came a voice from behind Alex.

Alex whirled around and found his uncle standing there. He could have hugged him.

"It's for his own safety," the officer said, but Alex could see him flushing. He hadn't expected to be confronted by an adult.

"Well, that's silly. These girls are harmless, and they'll help Alex take his mind off his problems."

Reluctantly, the officer stepped to the side and let the girls come up the steps and into the house.

Alex ushered them into the den and asked his uncle to join them. As they sat down he closed the window, turned the radio on and faced them from the computer chair.

"I wouldn't be surprised if the whole house is bugged," he whispered. He nodded at the radio. "That will cover up our conversation."

They all stared at him, speechless.

"I have a rough idea where Tanner is," he said, still whispering.

"Then why haven't you told the police?" his uncle asked quietly.

"Because it's possible one of them may be taking bribes from Hap."

Alex watched his uncle turn pale.

"It makes sense, doesn't it?"

His uncle shook his head helplessly. "Nothing should surprise me anymore."

"Even Dr. Montgomery inadvertently helped Hap out."

"No way."

Alex nodded.

"So where is Tanner?"

He leaned toward them and whispered even more quietly. "On the waterfront, in the city. Somewhere east of Canada Place. He seems to be in a warehouse, or even under a warehouse, if that makes sense. It's dark where he is and he's just above the water."

His uncle sat up. "I remember seeing a story on the news about all the homeless people who lived under the docks and warehouses on the water. There are ledges down there where they can camp out and where no one will bother them."

"That must be it!" Alex said. "He was also sending me pictures of Grouse Mountain, but I think that had to do with something else. He was trying to tell me a story, I think."

"What was the story?"

"Something about Hap overpowering me there. I don't know. It was weird. But then something happened and now I'm sure he's down on the waterfront."

"So what do you want us to do?" Zoe asked. Her eyes lit up at the thought of being involved in Tanner's rescue.

"I want you to go down there, phone Officer Russell on his cellphone and tell him to meet you there by himself. Explain to him everything I just told you. Then find Tanner!"

Mr. Bradshaw cleared his throat. "They could just phone him from one of their homes."

Alex shook his head. "Even with a cellphone there's a chance someone will overhear the conversation. He needs to hear this in person, and besides, if he has to come all the way out here, we'll be losing valuable time."

"Then I better go with the girls, Alex," said Mr. Bradshaw. "I can't just let them go on their own."

"I need you to stay here with me, Uncle John. I don't trust that cop at the front door."

Mr. Bradshaw stared at him, the truth sinking in. "The phone calls in and out of here are probably being monitored," he said.

"I figured as much," Alex whispered. "That's why we can't phone Officer Russell now."

"When you leave here," Alex told the girls, "go directly to the pay phone on the corner and call a cab. Have it take you to Canada Place and phone Officer Russell from there." He handed them the number.

"Stay put until he arrives. Tell him what I just told you and then let him take over."

Mr. Bradshaw took his wallet out of his back pocket. He pulled out four twenty-dollar bills. "This is for cab fare to and from the waterfront."

Alex looked at Caitlin. "Do you think you can do this?" he asked softly. She nodded.

They all stood up and Alex hugged both the girls before they left the den. He stood with the officer on the front steps while they walked down the road and around the corner. He remained standing there just a little longer, wanting to give the girls enough time to hire a cab and get away in case this officer had any ideas of sending someone after them. When he felt sufficient time had gone by, he looked the officer straight in the eye.

"Your little friends didn't stay long," the man said with a barely masked sneer.

Alex held his eyes a long time. "Maybe they didn't like the company." He turned and went inside.

twenty-nine

"Who are you?" Tanner asked. His eyes were growing accustomed to the thin light, and he could see figures sprawled out on the labyrinth of beams that lay horizontal above the water.

"Shh."

Pounding feet could be heard running above them. The boards creaked as the feet stomped directly overhead. Then they passed without slowing.

"He's gone, for now," said the person who'd pulled them through the hole.

Tanner peered at his rescuer, a fellow with threadbare, ragged clothing. Startling sky-blue eyes sparkled in a face that was black — black by birth or grime, Tanner couldn't tell. The guy smiled at him, knowing he was being sized up, and Tanner saw a mouthful of brown, decaying teeth.

"Who are you?" Tanner asked again.

"Just a fellow human being," he shrugged, "or street bum, depending on your perspective."

"You live down here?"

"Mostly up in the empty warehouses, but we can move

around down here without being noticed."

Tanner squinted into the shadows. "How long have you been here?"

"Five years, give or take a few." He scratched at his matted dreadlocks. "I'm probably the oldest. Most of the kids don't last as long as me." He gestured at the rotting beams and planks around them. "It may not be as cozy as the home you come from, but we're a community. We look out for one another and share what we have." He laughed derisively. "Which is, as you can see, very little. But the cops don't get down here much and it feels safer then sleeping in them parks or under noisy bridges."

They were street kids, Tanner realized, looking around, part of the almost invisible homeless community that lived in every big city. Vancouver was unique in that it had this vast dock system with abandoned warehouses that could be used for shelter.

Tanner saw Maureen slump against a beam and then slide into a crouching position. A startled rat scurried away.

"My friend here is sick," he said anxiously. "I need to get help for her."

"You're free to do whatever you want," the skinny guy said. Hunching over so he wouldn't scrape his head, he moved across the wooden beams to a corner where some plywood had been laid out to make a flimsy deck. A stack of old newspapers formed a mattress, and he sprawled himself out on it. "But I sense the man that's after you means business. He's had your friend up there for quite awhile."

"You knew she was there all this time?"

"Of course."

"Then why didn't you do something for her?"

He shrugged. "Down here we don't stick our noses into other people's business."

"But she was being held hostage!"

"So? No need to risk my neck only to find out she had what was coming to her. Down here you learn there's certain rhythms in life you don't tamper with, like cause and effect, and what-goes-around-comes-around — you know the ones I mean."

Tanner stared at him. Then he looked around at the six or seven teenagers squatting on the framework of the underside of this dock. They stared blankly back at him.

"Then why did you pull *me* down here?" he asked quietly.

"When it comes to kids I make exceptions. I still have a heart, even if I don't have a home." He stroked a tabby cat that had crept up from the shadows to curl against him. "Kids and cats," he mused. "I hope I don't live to regret it."

"How old are you?" Tanner asked suddenly.

"About nineteen. I've lost track." He saw Tanner's expression and laughed. "Yeah, I know. You age a bit quicker when you're exposed to the elements."

"So what do you suggest I do now?" Tanner asked.

"Is someone, besides that man, gonna be looking for you?"

"Yeah."

"Where will they be looking?"

"Maybe here, by now. They've probably figured it out."

"Then I'd just sit tight, if I was you, and think positive thoughts. The word will be out among the kids that you're here. If the right people come looking for you, they'll find you." He stroked the cat again. "And I've heard that positive thoughts can produce miracles."

Tanner regarded his rescuer with skepticism. He not only looked much older than he was, he talked older too. Maybe you do acquire a quirky kind of wisdom living on the street, he thought. He looked at Maureen. Her eyes were closed and she was breathing rapidly. He squatted down beside her and she leaned against him. He thought again about what this guy had just told him. Would Alex find him here? It seemed unlikely, yet he couldn't risk going above ground again. Not yet. If he ran into Max he'd be dead.

He looked around at his peculiar surroundings and pushed another picture of it to Alex. Then he began to focus on the idea of a rescue. He'd never considered the power of positive thinking before, but if he and Alex could send each other mental pictures ... Besides, it was the only thing left for him to do right now.

thirty

Alex paced about the house. He thought about getting something to eat, then realized he wasn't hungry. His uncle was trying to read the newspaper. His mom was trying to sleep. He felt sick at the thought of seeing Tanner's parents that afternoon. He knew their anxiety would only make him feel worse.

The front door was open to let a breeze through, and Alex again made eye contact with the officer standing there. He smiled, but Alex turned away. He hated adults who treated kids decently only when there were other adults watching. That was how this man had behaved. He'd ordered Dr. Montgomery to leave when his mom and uncle weren't around and he'd only let the girls in when his uncle had insisted on it. Once again, Alex decided to trust his instincts. He went into his bedroom, reached into his night table for the familiar pepper spray canister and slipped it into his pocket.

The front-door officer's cellphone rang.

"Hello?"

Alex wandered back down the hall and stood behind the open front door so he could better hear the one-sided conversation.

"You're kidding! Where'd they go?"

They? Who was he talking about?

"Unbelievable. You're right. We'll pick up the pace. I'll get him there now." Alex heard him snap his phone shut, knock once and then enter the house. He jumped when Alex stepped out from behind the door. Then his face flushed.

"That was your buddy, Russell. He says to bring you down to the station."

"What for?"

"They've set up the plan."

"And what plan is that?" Alex's uncle asked. He came into the front entry and put his arm around Alex's shoulder.

"Well, I don't have the details, sir. I just know I have to follow my orders, which are to bring this boy down to the station."

"I think I'll phone Officer Russell and get that message confirmed," Alex said, "just to be sure there's been no mistake."

"I can assure you," the officer said, a hard edge to his voice, "there has been no mistake." He stood back so Alex could pass through the doorway. "Let's go, kid, into the car, pronto."

But Alex didn't budge and Mr. Bradshaw didn't loosen his grip on Alex's shoulder.

"You are interfering with my police work, sir," the police officer said, addressing Mr. Bradshaw. "Let go of the boy and step out of the way."

Alex was aware of the cool, thin canister tucked in his pocket, but he was equally aware of the holster and gun hanging from the cop's hip. By the time he pulled the pepper spray out of his pocket, twisted the top and clicked it twice, the gun would be pointing right at him.

Mr. Bradshaw hadn't loosened his grip, but Alex nodded. "Let me go, Uncle John. I'm sure he's just doing what he has to do to protect me." He shoved his hands into his pockets, feigning defeat. "I'll go."

But Mr. Bradshaw held firm.

"What's happening here?" asked Mrs. Swanson, emerging from her bedroom down the hall.

The officer spun around and smiled warmly at her. "Everything's fine, ma'am. I'm just taking Alex down to the station for his own protection."

Alex pulled himself free of his uncle's grip and walked past the officer to his mother. He pulled his clenched hand out of his pocket and gave her a hug. "I'll be safe there, Mom." He gripped her hands with his own and looked into her eyes, hard. He nodded. "I love you."

"I love you too, Alex." She also nodded slightly, as if answering an unspoken question. "Are you sure everything is okay?"

"Yeah, I'm sure."

He dropped her hands, which she quickly tucked into the pockets of her bathrobe. Then he turned to the officer. "I'm ready to go," he said, ignoring the look of concern on his uncle's face.

"Smart boy," the officer said, nodding. "After you." Once again, he moved so Alex could pass through the door first.

Alex's mom followed Alex and the officer down to the unmarked police car. John Bradshaw watched for a moment and then hurried back into the house. The officer opened the car door for Alex and waited while he hopped in. He swung the door shut and turned to speak again to Mrs. Swanson, who was standing right behind him. That's when he saw the small canister of pepper spray pointed directly at his face.

.... thirty-one

"Well, I do believe the power of positive thinking has worked once again," the voice said, laughing.

Tanner's eyes snapped open. He'd been sending pictures to Alex, but now found the fellow who'd rescued him from Max leaning over him. "What did you say?"

"Your help has come. There's an officer out there named Russell looking for you."

"How do you know?"

"I told you. Word gets around quickly on the water."

Tanner felt Maureen stir. He propped her against the beam beside him so he could stand up.

"I need to get to him."

"You will. He's being brought here as we speak."

There was a knock on the planks above them and then a board was pulled away, allowing a bright stream of sunlight to shine in. "The coast is clear," a voice said. "Tell them to come out and head west half a block. They'll find who they're looking for there."

The wise homeless person spoke sharply to Tanner. "You

heard him. Get going."

"How can I thank you?" Tanner whispered.

"I dunno. Make a donation to the soup kitchen. Send blankets. Whatever. But always remember the power of positive thinking."

Tanner hesitated. He felt he needed to say something more, but didn't know what.

"You're welcome," the young man snapped, reading his thoughts. "Now go, before the other guy returns!"

Tanner pulled Maureen up beside him and was grateful that she could still stand. With the homeless guy's help, he pushed her through the opening above them. Then he reached up and pulled himself through. The sunlight was blinding, but he kept moving, pulling Maureen along with him. He turned right when he reached the street and stumbled along for a few hundred feet. Maureen tripped and fell. He pulled her to her feet and tried heaving her over his shoulder. Suddenly, Officer Russell was standing in front of him, taking Maureen out of his arms. He guided Tanner into an idling car. Zoe was there, and so was Caitlin. Zoe leaned over and hugged him fiercely. Officer Russell called for an ambulance, and then called Alex's home.

"It's over, Tanner," Officer Russell said when he'd finished his call. He turned to face his passengers in the back of the car. "Hap's bail was revoked and he's just been arrested at the foot of Grouse Mountain." He paused, glancing at Maureen. "I understand he was hoping to lure Alex there somehow."

"I thought that's what he was doing!" Tanner said.

The officer cocked his head, puzzled, but continued. "When that didn't work, he tried to get Alex delivered to him there. And he was almost successful, but your brother is too smart!" He laughed. "He outsmarted him."

Maureen began to cough in the passenger seat beside him.

Officer Russell put his hand on her shoulder and waited until the coughing spell eased up before he continued.

"Apparently there was talk among Hap's people that he was trying to use the supernatural to abduct Alex. That created some concern. They thought he was getting desperate, which in turn caused his authority to be disputed and he began to lose control. I guess his loyal 'family' thought he'd lost his mind." Officer Russell winked at Tanner. "Suddenly there are lots of people willing to talk. They're hoping to get shown some leniency for stepping forward. We'll have lots of good witnesses." He glanced at Maureen, who seemed to be shaking less violently now. "Everything's going to be all right."

"What about Alex?" he asked.

"Alex is fine," the officer said. "He's a smart kid. Your parents are there too."

"How did you find me?"

"Well, Alex got your pictures, I guess, and told Zoe and Caitlin about them. He'd been told there might be a cop taking bribes from Hap, so he sent the girls down here to call me. I'm acquainted with the street kids down here, so I put out the word that I'd come to get you." He shook his head. "It didn't take long at all. There are some really good kids living here. Society has let them down." He sighed. "They've made a few bad choices — I'm not saying they're perfect — but no one deserves to live like that," he added.

The sound of an ambulance approaching spurred the officer into action. He hopped out of the car and flagged it down. Then he opened the door on the side where Maureen sat shaking and helped the paramedics get her into their van. Tanner told them what he knew about her condition, and they pulled away, sirens blaring again.

"There're a lot of questions you need to answer, Tanner, but I'll take you home now. I suspect you'll continue to be under careful police protection until after the trial, but I think the worst is over."

Tanner sat back, flanked by Zoe and Caitlin, and closed his eyes. He pushed a picture of a trophy to his brother. Within seconds the trophy came back to him.

thirty-two

"I can't wait until the trial," Tanner said. He was sitting on one side of Maureen's hospital bed and Alex was on the other. A police officer stood watch at the door.

"Why's that?" Maureen asked.

"To see him get nailed."

"Apparently they have a rock-solid case against him and they've also arrested almost a dozen others, including Max and Kathy," Alex explained. "Everything was falling apart, just like Max told Tanner, and now everyone is ratting on everyone else."

"So what's this about you having to use your pepper spray too?" she asked Alex.

Alex laughed, remembering. "The guy who was assigned to protect me turned out to be working for both sides. He got a call at my house from Hap — after you guys escaped — and he was going to deliver me to him."

"Whoa."

"Whoa is right. I managed to hand the canister to my mom." He laughed. "Good thing she wasn't forced to use it, though. I'd never shown her how to work the trigger, but he didn't know that."

"What happened?"

"Mom was so cool. She just kept holding that pepper spray in his face. He was afraid to even breathe. My uncle had gone to get the backyard cop to come around to the front. That cop quickly confirmed that I wasn't supposed to be taken anywhere, and he took care of it from there."

"Was that the only bad cop?" Maureen asked.

"Yeah. It only takes one," Alex said.

"So, what are you going to do when you get out of here?" Tanner asked Maureen.

"I'm going to straighten my life out somehow," she said. "I've been thinking a lot about those kids who live in the empty warehouses."

"You're going to go live with them?"

"No," she laughed. "But I've been given a lucky break considering what I was involved in. I think maybe it's time to give something back to society now, you know?"

"Like what?"

"Well, perhaps I could help get kids off the street, and keep them off."

"Yeah, like you got me off the streets?" Alex asked.

She smiled sheepishly. "Like I told Tanner, Alex, you've got to be stupid to get hooked, and then you get even stupider. I was into it big time back then, and I'll never forgive myself for what I did to you. But if I can help someone else stay off the street, maybe I can redeem myself somehow."

Alex's uncle appeared at the hospital room door.

"You ready to go, boys?" he asked.

Alex nodded, then turned back to Maureen. "Just make sure you're better by August 28. We're going to see Hap get convicted, and then we're going to party!"

"I'll be there," she said. Then she grinned. "But which one of you guys is going to be my date?"

....

On the night of August 27, Tanner's family, who were all in Vancouver for Hap's trial, and Alex's family, with the exception of his father, went out to dinner together. Zoe, Caitlin and Dr. Montgomery had been included in the pre-celebration, as had Officer Russell and Maureen. They'd been assured that the trial would be swift and decisive, so the mood in the private room of the Chinese restaurant was jubilant. When they'd finished eating, Alex's uncle stood up and clinked his water glass to get everyone's attention.

"This isn't a wedding, Uncle John," Tanner teased.

"Good point, Tanner," Mr. Bradshaw said, "and it's not Thanksgiving, either. But I feel that with us all gathered like this tonight, it's a good time to reflect on the past year, count our blessings and discuss our future. We may not have the opportunity to get together like this after the trial, so this is as good a time as any."

The room grew quiet while they waited for Mr. Bradshaw to continue.

He cleared his throat. "As you know, Alex and Tanner are the catalysts here. It's because of them that we're all together tonight."

The brothers glanced at each other, wondering where he was going with this.

"Alex has always been a very special nephew to me," Mr. Bradshaw continued, "even during the years where we'd lost touch with one another. I love him like my own son."

Alex nodded and raised his water glass in a salute. "It goes both ways, Uncle John," he said, his voice sounding thick in his throat.

"And Tanner," Mr. Bradshaw continued, "is, as you know, Alex's brother, and over the summer I've had the good fortune to get to know him." He turned and spoke directly to Tanner. "I'd just like to say, son, that you're every bit as much family as Alex is. Come see us as often as you can."

Tanner pushed his chair back and walked to the head of the long table where Alex's uncle stood. They shook hands, and then Mr. Bradshaw put his arm around Tanner's shoulder and held him close. He cleared his throat before he continued.

"As you all know, Tanner set out to find their birth parents this summer, particularly their birth mother."

Tanner flushed and his gaze dropped down to his feet.

"And he didn't get the results he was hoping for. Their birth mother died, and no one knows who their biological father is, but I'm going to make this commitment to you, Tanner." He turned to face him. "I'm going to attempt to track down your biological grandparents and perhaps they'll be willing to share some information with you about your birth mother."

Tanner reached out and hugged the older man. Then he turned to address the group. "I would, um, I would just like to apologize," he stammered, "for putting you all through hell this summer. Especially," he said, "my parents, Uncle John and Alex's mom, Pat."

"What about me, Tanner?" Zoe asked.

"And me," said Officer Russell.

"And me," Caitlin added.

Suddenly everyone was shouting "and me" and Tanner laughed, realizing the futility of trying to keep the mood serious. He shook his head, grinning, and went back to his chair.

Mr. Bradshaw clinked his glass again and waited for the room to grow quiet once more. He took a deep breath.

"There's a silver lining in every situation, and I think the boys have learned something this summer about what a family really is. Just tonight Dr. Montgomery was telling me that he's always believed family ties exist beyond physical presence.

That's why he's so fascinated by the boys' unusual gifts, but I think that theory could be extended. Alex recently received a letter from his father." Mr. Bradshaw pulled a sheet of paper out of his pocket. "And he said I could share with you the following quote from it." He began to read.

You told me, Alex, that there were ways for me to deal with my problem. Until that moment I'd never admitted to myself that I had one. It was a shock, coming from you, but hearing those words made me finally own up to the fact that I do.

So I have found help. I'm receiving anger management counseling and I've started going to Alcoholics Anonymous. I haven't had a drink in two weeks and I've already learned that the anger I vented on you was really displaced anger I felt for myself.

I'm sorry for the misery I've put you through, but it was never because I didn't love you. I always have. I always will.

The room was perfectly still.

"So you see," Mr. Bradshaw continued, "Alex may not be with his father, but Frank is feeling Alex's presence with him anyway. And it's giving him the strength to turn his life around."

Maureen began clapping very softly. Then Officer Russell joined in. One by one everyone in the room joined in, everyone except Alex and his mother. He looked at her, she nodded, and eventually they began to clap too.

"I hope Frank feels our positive thoughts with him tonight, wherever he is," Mr. Bradshaw said, over the sound of the applause.